T-19572

SO-COL-871

DATE DUE			

Not Just A Summer Crush

Adler, C. S.

AR

Lex: 650   R.L: 5.1   Pts: 8

Not Just a
Summer Crush

Not Just a Summer Crush

C.S. ADLER

Clarion Books • New York

Clarion Books
a Houghton Mifflin Company imprint
215 Park Avenue South, New York, NY 10003
Text copyright © 1998 by Carole S. Adler

Text is set in 13/16.5 Ehrhardt

Printed in the U.S.A.

Library of Congress Cataloging-in-Publication Data

Adler, C. S. (Carole S.)
Not just a summer crush / C.S. Adler.
p.   cm.
Summary: A Twelve-year-old girl develops a crush on her English teacher
when he spends a week at a beach near her family's cottage.
ISBN: 0-395-88532-9
[1. Teachers—Fiction. 2. Family life—Fiction. 3. Beaches—Fiction.] I. Title.
PZ7.A26145No1998
[Fic]—dc21
98-11358
CIP   AC

BP 10 9 8 7 6 5 4 3 2 1

For my newest grandchild, Julia Bryn.
Welcome, and may your life be as full of delight
as your coming is to our whole family.
—With love, Grandma Carole

Not Just a
Summer Crush

Chapter 1

Hana pulled on last year's swimsuit with ease. Her body was still salamander-small and slender. Small enough to slip past the family and get to the beach before they appended her to one of their plans? She could hear the five of them at the breakfast table. Alan was mocking Elena's yogurt diet and Mom was pigeon-cooing at them to keep the peace. Dad's irritated rumble caused a sudden silence, until Eric, the eldest, changed the mood and subject.

Now, Hana told herself. She ran soundlessly in her bare feet for the front door. In her hands, she was clutching her book and towel, all the beach equipment she needed.

"Hana!" Mom's voice stopped Hana at the screen door. "Where do you think you're going?"

"To Grandma's beach." Hana could feel five pairs

of eyes on her. "That's what Grandma lent us her cottage for, isn't it?" she asked them. "So we could use the beach?" She shrank under their uncomprehending gazes. "I mean," she said, "we've been here two days and nobody's even gone to see if it's still there."

"You've gone, haven't you, Hana?" her brother Alan asked.

"I went to see the sunset. And—"

"So, is it still there?" Alan persisted.

Hana nodded, unwilling to give him more than that small gesture. Alan didn't need much of an excuse to make a fool out of her.

"Well, good. Then the rest of us are saved from having to check it out," he said.

"It's not much of a beach, Hana," Mom said. The damp July air had made Mom's hair curl like a poodle's. She gave Hana a kind smile and continued. "When you were little, we used it because the water's so shallow. But think of all the beautiful beaches around here we can go to now."

"Hana likes Grandma's beach because she ate half of it as a baby," Elena said. Her smirk seemed to be put on with her makeup in the morning.

"Come on, guys. Leave the kid alone," Eric told them. Still in solemn, eldest-brother mode, he took it on himself to answer Hana. "We've got two weeks here, mouse. We don't have to hit the sand every single day to get our money's worth out of the place."

"Eric, you know Grandma doesn't charge us," Mom said.

"It's just an expression, Mother," he said patiently. "Come on, Alan. We're wasting time. Are you coming to town with me or not?"

Alan swigged the rest of his outsized glass of orange juice and stood up to stretch. His fingertips touched the low ceiling.

"Alan, don't do that. It leaves marks," Mom said. She said it every morning because Alan did it every morning.

"Sorry." Alan swiped a kiss at his mother's cheek, and he and Eric were out the door faster than a pair of wind-up toys. They were biking into town for—they claimed—a basketball game with summer friends.

So long as they could use their bikes or walk to get there, seventeen-year-old Eric and not-quite-sixteen-year-old Alan could go where they pleased. And Elena, at fifteen, usually got what she wanted, which today was to go shopping in Orleans with Mom. On the way, Mom was going to drop Dad off at his fishing buddy's house. Of course, no one questioned Dad's right to fish because that was his only form of relaxation. As for Hana, being the youngest, what she got was to do as she was told.

"Hana, hurry and put some shorts on. You can't go with us like that," Mom said. The car horn was honking outside to signal that Dad had finished loading his fishing gear and wanted to leave.

"Why do I have to go? I won't get into any trouble on Grandma's beach," Hana argued.

"You're only twelve," Mom said. "I don't think—"

"You let Elena go places alone when *she* was twelve," Hana said.

"Well, but Elena . . ." Mom hesitated to say what Hana knew she thought—that her youngest daughter was still a baby while Elena had been a grown woman as soon as she got out of diapers.

"Oh, let her stay, Mom," Elena put in. "Hana couldn't get in trouble if she tried. Look, she's got a book with her, for heaven's sake."

Mom's eyes fell on the book. Something about it seemed to reassure her because she launched into her usual warnings about swimming close to shore and being sure to use enough sunscreen. Dad honked again. Mom put her hand to her cheek. "Oh, I don't know, though," she said. "We'll be gone the whole morning. . . ."

"Mom, Hana likes being alone," Elena coaxed.

"Come on. The sale will be all picked over if we don't hurry."

"But what about Hana's lunch? We're out of everything already. Don't forget, food shopping's what we really need to go to Orleans for, Elena."

The next blast of the horn lasted longer.

"There's peanut butter and crackers," Hana said quickly.

"That's all she lives on anyway." Elena took their mother's hand, scooped up Mom's purse, and pulled her out the door, yelling, "We're coming, Daddy!"

Over her shoulder Mom asked, "Hana, would you do the breakfast dishes, please?"

Hana nodded and waved. As soon as they were gone, she went to work stacking the dishes in the dishwasher and wiping off the big table. That was a fair exchange for not having to spend the morning dragging along behind Elena and Mom through every boring shop in Orleans.

Instead, Hana had been granted a crystalline morning on the tiny patch of harbor beach. There, she could curl into a hollow in the sand and read, blanketed by the warmth of the sun. She locked the sliding door, hid the key under the clamshell, and set off. It was shady walking between the autumn olive, scrub oak, and bayberry bushes that filled Grandma's backyard. Once she reached Indian Neck Road, though, the walk became hot and sunny. But she only had a couple of hundred feet to go before she came to the entrance to the beach.

Elena's remark about Hana's liking to be alone had left a bad aftertaste. For one thing, it wasn't true. She might be quiet, but Hana liked being around people—her family, friends. She even missed her bossy grandmother, who was off at an Elderhostel program in Kentucky this week.

How typical of Elena to believe she understood her younger sister without ever once bothering to ask Hana how she felt about life, or about *anything* important. Just because she was small and the youngest, nobody in her family thought she was much. If she had a woman's body, like fifteen-year-old Elena had, would they respect her more? Probably. Better yet if she were a boy. Her brothers bulldozed their way through the family as they pleased, so long as they stayed out of real trouble.

Even so, Hana didn't want to be a boy, and she didn't want to be big-boned and weight conscious like Elena, who was always on a diet. She liked being small. Most of the time she was glad that she could slip through spaces and watch what was going on without being observed. She might not say much, but she thought a lot, as they'd find out if they ever listened to her.

"Hana's the afterthought," Eric had once told a friend of his when he didn't know Hana was listening. "The folks planned on three kids. And then they had her."

It was lonely being odd man out in the family.

There was only one car in the small sand parking area. Good. The bandanna-sized beach wouldn't be crowded. Sun shimmered invitingly on the calm water and the tide was near high. So Hana decided to go for a leisurely swim before settling into the lap of her book. A man sat on the flat rock in the middle of the small breakwater that was Hana's favorite drying-off spot. No matter; the man would probably be gone by the time she finished swimming. She flexed her toes in the damp, yielding sand and sniffed deep of the faint seaweedy smell that came off the wet brown vegetation at the high tide mark. All winter, when she daydreamed in classes, she would be sniffing for the salt tang in the air and thinking of this humble dab of sand.

She dropped her flip-flops, put her book on top of them, and set the towel atop both, thereby protecting the book top and bottom. The water was warm today, as warm as the pond, and she didn't have to ease her way into its silky greenness. She just dove in and came up wet. She was a dolphin, a seal, a silvery fish swimming from breakwater to breakwater, parallel to the shore. Her arms barely broke through the water's surface and her legs propelled her invisibly.

After a while, she rolled over on her back and narrowed her eyes at the hazy sun. Backstroking, she could feel its warmth on her stomach, but thin as she was, she could never swim for very long before her lips turned blue and her teeth began to chatter. She butterfly-kicked the rest of the way back to her end of the beach.

He was still there, the man on the rocks, staring out to Great Island as if he were memorizing its sinewy beige outline between sky and water.

"Go home," she muttered to herself, "and give me back my rock." She walked on the sand alongside the breakwater and frowned up at him.

He turned his head to look at her and she gasped. Mr. Crane! It was Mr. Crane, her sixth-grade teacher from back home in Schenectady! Her heart quivered and shrank painfully as she stared at him. His eyes had swung around to Great Island in the distance. He hadn't seen her. Or if he had, he hadn't recognized her with her stringy brown hair dripping like seaweed on her shoulders. But it had only been a month. Mid-June to mid-July. How could he have forgotten her already? She bit her lip, bent her head, and hurried to her towel.

Second choice in drying-off places was the wooden pilings that separated the beach from the cluster of rental cottages behind and above it. She wrapped her towel around her and leaned against the pilings.

He had forgotten her. The thought depressed her so much she didn't want to get her book and start reading. And it was *Julie of the Wolves*, one of her old favorites. Mr. Crane. He had told her she had an original mind. "Fresh and vivid turns of phrase," he'd written on her first composition, the one about waiting for Elena to get finished in the bathroom. Immediately, Hana had imagined how she would grow up and become a famous author and return to school—where he'd still be teaching, with little crinkles beside his seaweed-colored eyes and his mouth quirking up when some kid's behavior struck him as funny. Although by then he'd have had to learn how to put the kid down with a frown instead.

"You were my favorite teacher ever," she would tell him.

"You were my favorite student," he would say, recognizing her at once.

She would reach out her hand to him. They wouldn't need words to understand each other. He would smile. She would smile back. The warmth of their fingers would blend and they would forget to let go.

Seaweed-colored eyes. The notion wasn't romantic. Well, he wasn't a handsome man, not cute the way the girls said the gym teacher was. But he was gentle and she liked his thinness and the soft waves of his light brown hair. Oh, Mr. Crane! Surely if she put on one of her school outfits from sixth grade, he would remember her. Because he'd given her an A and she'd dropped a note on his desk telling him what a good teacher he was before she'd run out the door on the last day of school.

He couldn't have gotten many notes like that. Most of the kids mocked him, and some were mad at him for not keeping order in the class. Katie Banks had complained that she couldn't concentrate in Mr. Crane's class because it was too noisy and someone was always throwing spitballs. Anne McKay, who knew everything, had said she doubted Mr. Crane would be coming back next year. Hana breathed out a shuddering sigh.

Then she tensed. Mr. Crane, the Mr. Crane in the here and now, had stood up. He was walking off the rocks toward her. She dropped her head. But then she saw his naked toes in the sand, turned toward her. He'd stopped.

"Uh," he said uncertainly. "Uh, Hana?"

She flashed a look at him from under the wet strings of her hair.

"It *is* you," he said. "I thought the sea creature that passed me on the rocks looked familiar. Hi. It's Mr. Crane. Remember? Sixth grade?"

"Yes, I remember," she said. She swallowed. "Hi," she said.

He stretched, and she saw his ribs rise under his black T-shirt. Long bare legs stuck out below his baggy shorts. His legs were very white with fine brown hairs, as if they'd never been out in the sun before.

"You were in swimming," he said.

She nodded. "I swim here a lot."

He nodded back. "Umm. Well, then I'll see you again, probably. I'm here for a week. This is the beach my folks used to bring me to when I was a kid. Say, this isn't the one you described in your favorite place composition, is it?"

She nodded.

"Of course," he said. "I should have recognized it. That was a fine description. But you never said it was a beach in Wellfleet."

"I'm here for two weeks," she said, modestly pretending not to have heard his praise.

"I remember you wrote something about how the beach seems to change all the time." He nodded to himself as if he were pleased to have recalled at least one detail. "Well, now I can check that out, can't I?"

She pushed a smile out to raise the corners of her lips, just barely. But she couldn't risk speaking. Her heart was pounding so hard he might hear it.

"Well, good," he said finally. "So, see you around. Don't take any wooden nickels."

He began to walk away. Suddenly she heard herself ask, "Mr. Crane? What's a wooden nickel?"

He turned to look over his shoulder at her. Sure enough, one corner of his mouth quirked up adorably. "I don't know exactly," he said. "It's something my grandfather used to say to me, but I never thought to ask him. Do you suppose there ever were any? Wooden nickels, I mean?"

"I guess not."

"I guess not, too," he said, and he nodded and walked around the bulkhead into the parking area and out of sight.

Her heart slowed to a more sedate beat, although it took a while. Now what? Had she been so awkward a conversationalist that he would find another beach in order to avoid talking to her? Or would she see him again? And if she did, what could she say? She would have to think of some topics to talk to him about in case. Maybe she should write them down. What might he be interested in? Books?

"Oh, Mr. Crane!" Hana spoke her longing out loud. A longing that had been given a new charge by this unexpected meeting.

Chapter 2

Hana was daydreaming about Mr. Crane while she lunched on crackers and peanut butter at the big table that about filled Grandma's glassed-in porch. Suddenly, her long-legged brothers burst into the cottage.

"Anybody home?" Alan asked her.

"Just me," she said.

"Good," Alan said to his brother. "Nobody's home. Now's our chance to get it fixed before they find out."

"Find out what?" Hana asked.

"None of your business, mousy." Alan ruffled the damp ribbons of Hana's brown hair and took a swipe of peanut butter from the jar before galloping down to the basement.

Eric followed, carrying a paper bag from the hardware store. "It's just that old washing machine," he said over his shoulder to Hana.

Probably they'd tried to wash a load of sneakers again. The machine had broken loose from its connections before, after bouncing around the concrete floor with a load of their sneakers. Mr. Crane wouldn't cause trouble like that. He was neat. Every day he had come to school in a shirt and tie—no jacket. But his shirt had always been ironed. Did his mother iron it for him? Hana knew he didn't have a wife because the bolder girls had asked him that the first day of sixth grade when they'd seen how young he was.

Of course, he could live with a girlfriend who ironed. Unless he lived alone and did his own ironing. That would be the most interesting explanation. Probably he had a girlfriend, though. Was she pretty? Even if she didn't iron for him, she'd be pretty, Hana was sure. Wives sometimes weren't—like in the supermarket—but girlfriends always were. If he had a girlfriend, she could have come to Wellfleet with him. So why had he been alone on the beach, then?

"Hana." It was Alan, the operator, back again. "Can you lend us ten bucks?"

"No," she said.

"Why not? You have it. I know you do because you never spend a dime of your allowance."

"Yes, she does. On books," Eric said. He was standing behind Alan, who had crouched in front of Hana to persuade her face to face.

"But you have ten bucks. I know because I looked in your purse," Alan said.

"You keep out of my stuff, Alan," Hana said. "And you can't have any money because last time you didn't pay me back."

"What do you mean? I always pay you back. Don't I, Eric?" He turned his handsome face toward his long-jawed older brother.

"Not always." Eric folded his arms and leaned against the wall, ready to wait until Alan had succeeded in persuading her.

"You borrowed twenty-six dollars in June to buy your girlfriend a present. Remember?" Hana said. She'd prepared this argument for the next time he wanted to borrow money from her. Now that time had come. But she hated fighting, and the nerves bunching up under her skin were making her frantic. Fighting sometimes upset her so much that she threw up.

"And I paid you back. I know I did," Alan said with such sincerity in his yellowy cat's eyes that she almost believed him.

Still she shook her head, even as she asked herself, "Could he have?" No—if he had, she would have more money in her wallet. She hadn't put anything in her savings account in months. No, he *couldn't* have paid her back. He was just a liar, and how could she fight a liar?

"Listen, Hana. If you say I didn't pay you back, I believe you," Alan said. "So I will—as soon as I get some cash. Okay? Meanwhile, you have to lend Eric and me ten bucks so we can buy another connection for the hose for this stupid washing machine. . . . Unless you'd rather we tell Dad you broke it."

"He wouldn't believe you."

"No. He wouldn't," Eric said bitterly. "Anything broken has to be our fault."

Alan rolled his lower lip out and trained his eyes trustingly on Hana. "You like hearing Dad yell at us?" he asked her.

"No," she said, squirming while a minute passed and their eyes held her hostage. "Oh, all right," she said. "But you better pay me back, and what you borrowed in June, too."

"Right. Twenty dollars, wasn't it?"

"Twenty-six. I wrote it down so I wouldn't forget this time."

Eric snorted. "You think she's still little enough to fool into believing a nickel's worth more than a dime because it's bigger, Alan?"

"Hey, no." Alan rolled out flat on the floor and

did a backward flip. Then he crouched in front of Hana again. "Come on. I'm not trying to con you, Hana baby. But don't we do you favors? Like who drives you wherever you want to go?"

"Mom, usually," Hana said.

"Hana never wants to go anywhere," Eric said.

"Whose side are you on, brother?" Alan asked in irritation.

"She already said she'd give us the ten," Eric pointed out. "How about we write you an IOU this time, Hana?"

"Fine." She was weary of the argument.

"Done. I knew we could count on you, half-pint." Alan rose straight up to full height without seeming to bend anything. He had been a gymnast for three years.

She gave them the money and they rushed off to get their bikes for the trip to the hardware store.

Hana's father came in while she was making her list of things to talk about with Mr. Crane if she should see him again. "Anybody home?" Dad asked.

"Just me. Where's Mom and Elena?"

"Still shopping. I got a ride home with Jim Henry's neighbor. Jim's boat's out of commission so we had to put off the fishing trip. What's for lunch?"

"Peanut butter, until Mom does the food shopping."

"That'll be if she has time after she finishes buying out the clothing stores for your sister. One good thing about you, Hana. You don't cost me much. . . . Yet."

He shambled over to the refrigerator, his bulk matching its solidness and height. "Not even any leftovers from dinner. Boys must have finished them before they went to bed last night."

He got a can of soup out of the pantry, looked at it gloomily, and returned to the refrigerator for a bottle of beer. She guessed the aborted fishing trip had disappointed him a lot. He worked such long hours in his construction business that the only time he had for fishing was during the two weeks of vacation he took.

"Did you have any luck last night, Dad?"

"Lost my best lure in the rocks. No fish left in these waters anyway. It's disgusting."

"Umm," she said.

"What'd you have for lunch?"

"Peanut butter."

He grimaced. "Figures that the one thing I hate would be the only one we never run out of." He returned the soup can to the pantry, opened the beer, and drank half of it thirstily. Then he settled on the couch facing the TV in the living room. A tennis match was on the sports channel. He began watching it with glum disinterest.

She'd ask Mr. Crane about school and what grade he was going to teach next year, Hana decided. And shells—she'd tell him she had found angel wings on the harbor beach, and boat and jingle shells, oyster and clam. So the shelling hadn't gotten nearly as bad as people said.

"Hi, Dad. You catch anything?" It was Alan, back with Eric, who was already halfway down to the basement with another little brown bag from the hardware store. Alan stood talking to his father, blocking his view of the basement steps. No doubt Alan was chatting deliberately to distract Dad from what Eric might be doing down there, Hana thought.

"No boat. No fishing."

"Maybe you ought to try one of those sport fishing boats that take you way out," Alan said.

"Costs too much. Not worth it."

"Yeah, it is, Dad. You work hard enough that you deserve to live it up on your vacation."

"Yeah," their father said. "Some vacation. There isn't even any food in this shack."

"Want me to fry you up some eggs?"

"No, that's okay. Your mother should be home soon."

"Not if she's shopping with Elena. You know how that girl is. She's probably trying on everything she can squeeze into."

A clang from the basement made their father look toward the door. "What was that?"

"Nothing. Eric's got some project going. He's just like you, Dad. Got to keep busy all the time."

It was lucky for the brothers that before their father's suspicions were roused enough for him to get up and investigate, Mom came in loaded down with supermarket shopping bags. "Traffic was awful from the drive-in on," she said. "It must have taken us fifteen minutes to go a mile. . . . Sorry about your friend's boat, Vergil. He told me when I went to pick you up."

"You get anything in the way of deli?" Dad asked.

"Of course. I'll make you a sandwich right now if you're hungry."

"I'll make my own." He rose stiffly from the couch. "Just give me the stuff I need."

Sunsets, Hana wrote down. Ask Mr. Crane if he likes them and tell him about the spectacular purple and pink one reflecting off the water the night we arrived. It had been special enough to fix in the memory bank of beautiful moments that she was amassing to draw on in bad times.

"Hana, I bought you a new bathing suit," Mom said.

"You did?" Hana's heart sank. Mom always picked babyish things for her. She hoped it wouldn't have a ruffle. Mom thought a ruffle across her chest hid the fact that Hana was so flat. Hana expected that she might be reduced to wearing a chest ruffle for the rest of her life. Her grandmother was skinny and flat chested, and the Aunt Hana for whom she was named had been, too, judging from photos of her.

"Poor Hana," Mom always said when she looked at pictures of her dead sister. If Hana had been pathetic, why had Mom wanted to name her youngest daughter after her, Hana had asked once. Mom had been so hurt that she refused to answer. "Poor Hana." It was like a curse.

Hana wondered when Mr. Crane was likely to return to the beach. Not this afternoon. Probably not ever because surely he had a car. With a car, he could go to any beach he wanted. And this afternoon it would be low tide. Grandma's beach at low tide *was* kind of mucky. Hana only preferred it then because she got nauseous going to the ocean beach stuffed in the backward-facing seat of the station wagon with all the beach equipment.

Besides, walking to Grandma's beach alone felt like freedom. It was one of the few places Mom let her go alone. But neither of those reasons for tolerating the muckiness of low tide applied to Mr. Crane. Unless he had liked sitting on the rocks. He

22

might want to go back and sit there again to think. To think about what? Hana could ask him that if she dared. Maybe tonight when she went to check out the sunset. Maybe then he'd be there.

Chapter 3

The swimsuit had a pink and green ruffle, but at least it was black and it did fit well. Hana decided she could hide it under one of her brothers' old T-shirts until she got to the water. She thanked her mother and politely admired Elena's colorful new shorts and tops, secretly glad she was too thin to fit into many of her older sister's castoffs.

"Why don't you wear your new suit and come to the pond with us?" Mom asked her. "It'll be just you, Elena, and me. Your father's planning to prune Grandma's overgrown bushes, and the boys are biking to the ocean beach."

"I think I'll just hang out on Grandma's beach," Hana said.

"It's low tide," Mom said. "You know that beach is no good at low tide. What's the matter with you,

Hana? Don't you like your mother and sister any-more?"

"Oh, Mom, you know I love you."

"Then come to the pond with us."

"Mom's going to feel bad if you don't come, Hana," Elena said.

So Hana went. But the conversation in the front seat of the car was about dieting, and by the time they reached the pond, Hana had escaped into a day-dream. It featured Mr. Crane and an old English ballad he had read to her class about young lovers dying, but she changed the ending to leave the young lovers alive in each other's arms.

That evening, after she had finished drying the pots and pans Elena had washed, Hana announced firmly that she was going to the beach.

"To see the sunset?" Mom asked. "I'll go with you as soon as my game show's over."

"The sunset will be gone by then, Mom," Elena said for Hana.

"Why don't *you* go with your sister, Elena," Mom suggested. She disliked letting Hana go out alone close to dark.

"And get eaten alive by bugs? Not me," Elena said.

"She's got to preserve her peaches-and-cream complexion, don't you know?" Alan said with a fake

British accent. "One can hardly blame the girl, when it's all she's got."

"Won't he ever say anything nice to me?" Elena asked Mom.

"Didn't I just say she has nice skin? What's wrong with that?" Alan asked in his own voice.

"I'm leaving," Hana muttered. She pulled her favorite old sweater off the peg behind the front door and slipped out unnoticed as Dad began a rumbled complaint that his family fought too much.

". . . You kids don't know how lucky you are to have each other. When I was a boy, my only companion was a dog so old I had to carry him outside to do his business. If I'd had a brother or sister, I'd have treated him or her right, believe you me."

That sounded reasonable to Hana, but the only other family she knew from first-hand experience was her friend Katie Banks's. Katie and her brother and sister fought and teased each other continually, too. Dad had been an only child. He and Mom must have expected that two boys and two girls would be the ideal recipe for family happiness. Hana wondered how it would be if she were an only child. Would she be listened to then? But even if her parents listened, they'd never understand. Their perspectives were too different from hers; they looked out while she looked in. And neither of them cared much about sunsets.

A mockingbird flashed the white stripes under its wings as it dipped from the phone line to the pointy top of a juniper. The hush of evening had sealed off the rough edges of the landscape, softening everything. Hana could never decide whether early morning or evening was best. She'd have to ask Mr. Crane which he preferred. That would be a good question, sort of neutral and yet revealing. If there had been an evening star in view, she would have wished on it. "Let him be at the beach." But the sky was too light for stars, or even planets, to be visible.

She pulled her sweater on as she walked. It might be pilled and shapeless, but the wool was bunny soft and no new sweater could replace it. The temperature had already dropped from its afternoon high of eighty to sixty now that the sun was low on the horizon. The tide would be getting high again by now. What if he had been there all afternoon and she had missed him by going to the pond with Mom and Elena? She'd finished her book at the pond, and she'd swum all the way to the narrows with Mom. She'd even told Mom about Mr. Crane. Sort of.

"I met my teacher on the beach this morning," she'd said to her mother while they were rubbing themselves dry with the vivid pink and purple fish-print beach towels.

"Did you, dear? Which teacher?"

"Mr. Crane, my English teacher."

"Oh, yes, he was your favorite. So what did he say?"

"Not much. He's staying near the beach."

"Well, that's nice. I mean that you got to see him again." Mom had stretched out, stomach down, on her damp beach towel. "I think I'll take a little nap," she'd said, and yawned. "Shopping with Elena wears me out." A minute later she'd fallen asleep, and Hana had let herself sink into her book.

That evening the water was *so* high up on the sand that it licked at the bulkhead in places. The water's rumpled edge was piled here and there with sudsy froth that looked like detergent but was only some kind of natural biological effect. At least that's what the health department in town had assured Mom when she phoned about it. With so little room on the sand, nobody was there to watch the sunset. Probably they'd be down at the larger beach at the end of the peninsula, Hana thought—the other people and Mr. Crane as well.

The big beach area was only a little over half a mile down the road, but Hana didn't feel like going. The bluff between the road and the beach hid the sunset, and by the time she reached the parking lot at the end, she'd have missed it altogether. Anyway, Mr. Crane might not care about sunsets. He might be watching TV for all she knew—with his girlfriend, or his fiancée, or some other adult companion. It was really too much to hope that he had come here alone.

Hana crouched with her back against a dry bulkhead watching the red disk slide neatly into the slot between Chequesset Neck and the sky. Not much color around the sun, but there were enough wisps of clouds so that there might be an afterglow. She was watching for it and didn't realize anyone had come until he spoke.

"I should have guessed you'd be a sunset watcher, Hana."

"Mr. Crane?" She sat bolt upright with a start. He was wearing jeans and a dark blue sweatshirt that advertised Wellfleet Oysters. His pale skin had been burnished by the sun and he looked almost handsome.

"You know, I was hoping I'd bump into you again," he said, hunkering down a few feet from her against the bulkhead.

Her insides wheezed in and out like an accordion to have him so close. She hoped he couldn't see through her skin.

"I realized you're just the right person to consult," Mr. Crane continued.

"To consult?" she asked breathlessly.

He nodded. If there was an afterglow, Hana never saw it that evening. Mr. Crane had her complete attention.

"Yeah, that's why I drove out to the Cape and took this place," Mr. Crane said. "I thought I needed to be alone and really think this thing through. See, I'm at a crisis point in my life. . . . What do you say, Hana? Want to give me some advice?" He smiled at her. "Don't look so scared. It's not that earthshaking. . . . Well, actually, it is to me."

"What is?"

"This thing that I have to decide. About teaching."

"Oh?"

"And you were my student, one of my best students, so maybe your point of view won't be typical, but—" He took a deep breath. "I want you to be totally honest with me, Hana. Can you be?"

She nodded, feeling as immobilized and terrified as a fly caught in amber might if a fly had feelings.

Something of her agitation must have showed in her face, because Mr. Crane frowned and asked uncertainly, "Well, do you mind if I tell you my secrets?"

"Mind? Oh, no."

"Okay, good." He leaned forward and tugged off his sneakers. He wasn't wearing any socks, and she stared at his long, white, bony toes, the same ones she had seen that morning. In all her imaginings about Mr. Crane, she'd never considered what his toes might be like. How personal, she thought, how intimate to be acquainted with those naked digits.

"My parents think I should do another year of teaching," he continued. "You know, the old business of climbing back on the horse after it's thrown you? They made me feel like a coward when I said I was going to quit."

"You're quitting teaching?"

He nodded and sighed. "It was an awful year for me, Hana. I hated it."

"Oh," she said. "But you were my best teacher."

"Was I really? You didn't notice anything? I mean, what did other kids say about me?"

She considered. If she told him the things she'd overheard in the halls and the lunchroom, he'd be hurt. She didn't want to hurt him, but he wanted her to be honest. "You should have been stricter, maybe," she said.

"I tried," he said. "They told me not to smile until Christmas, and I did try to act tough."

"Everybody knew you weren't," Hana said.

"You mean they saw it right away?"

"Well—" She thought back. "The first day of class you talked about how you wanted us to love reading and writing and how you'd listen to anything we had to say about improving your lessons."

"Wrong?"

"Yeah, because they figured you were a first-year teacher and they could get away with murder."

"Oh, boy! And I was being so careful to prove I was fair and open minded." He ran his fingers through his hair.

"And then you let everyone sit where they wanted the first week," Hana said.

"Right. *That* was to show I was treating them with respect."

"But then the second week you made them sit in rows."

"Because they were taking unfair advantage of the situation. I mean, I couldn't even make myself heard when I was trying to teach something."

"And then you yelled."

He winced as he remembered the moment. "I lost my cool. I was afraid the principal was going to walk in and see the class out of control and me just standing there helpless." He put his head in his hands. "You're right. I can't go back. I was a complete failure."

"No, Mr. Crane." She touched his arm in her concern, then yanked her fingers back as if she'd scorched them. "Kids liked the projects you made us do. They were interesting. You just needed to get their attention before you started things."

"And how was I supposed to do that? I don't have the magic look. Down the hall, Ms. Leslie was new to teaching, too, and she didn't have rowdy classes. They didn't talk back to her or act up in her room. She had the look." He imitated Ms. Leslie's piercing stare.

He was trying to be funny, but Hana didn't laugh. Even his imitation was a flop. "You sort of let them think they could act up," Hana said gently.

He groaned. "I can't go back, Hana. I can't face another class like the one I had last year."

But it hadn't been a bad class, she thought, just a normal mix of good kids and cutups. Rather than hit him with that judgment, she swallowed and asked, "So what are you going to do?"

He looked over at her and smiled. "Good question. I've got a friend out west who leads rafting expeditions. He said I could work with him."

"Would you like that?"

"Rafting? I've done it. It's okay. It's not a lifetime career, of course. I also play the saxophone pretty well. I used to think I'd enjoy making a living at that, but as my folks were quick to point out, saxophone players don't get paid vacations and sick leave and pensions." He chewed on his lip and raised an eyebrow. "I don't know. When I was in college, I was looking forward to being a teacher. I thought inspiring kids was a job with such value to society that I'd be proud to say I was a teacher."

"You did make it fun," Hana said encouragingly. "Remember the nature unit, when we worked with the science teacher, and we had to find information about our animal and write an article and then a story or poem about it. And then you got the art teacher in and we learned how to draw our animal? Everybody loved that unit."

"Yes. Yes, I know they did. Even Jonny Holden did some work. He got excited about wolves. I think he even read a book on the subject. I mean, I know he mostly copied book jackets, but I think he actually read *White Fang*, or part of it anyway."

"So isn't that being a good teacher?"

"I guess it would take a good teacher to make Jonny Holden do anything. Or maybe a lot of luck." He laughed. "Let's say I had my moments."

"Some kids liked you, Mr. Crane. Some kids said you were the best teacher they'd ever had." She hoped he wouldn't ask her for names. If he did, she'd have to say she couldn't think of any offhand besides her own. That would convince him he'd been a failure, or that she was stupid, and she didn't want him thinking that either.

"There really were kids who thought I was good?" he asked shyly. "I don't know. There's a lot about teaching that I like, at least in theory. It's exciting to try and make things interesting that were dull for me when I went to school. There's a satisfaction in motivating kids. But—"

"You'd have more fun rafting?"

He laughed again. "You're quite a girl, Hana, the best listener I've ever met. Thanks. I'm glad I consulted with you. You've been a big help."

"I have?"

"You certainly have." He stood up. "Want me to walk you home? It's getting dark."

"No, thanks," she said. "I just go across the road a ways. Bye, Mr. Crane."

"David," he said. "Call me David."

She didn't think she could, at least not yet. But she waved and turned and ran back to the cottage repeating his first name under her breath all the way. David, David, David. It made a lovely rhythm to run to.

Chapter 4

The next morning Hana stood in her old bathing suit brushing her teeth while she studied her face in the bathroom mirror. She didn't look like anybody else in the family. She didn't look like anybody much. Small eyes, small nose, small mouth—like a chipmunk or a squirrel, any chipmunk, any squirrel. No wonder Mr. Crane hadn't noticed her at first.

She reached hesitantly into the medicine cabinet where Elena kept her cosmetics and picked up a lipstick. Once when Hana had worn lipstick for a class play, Mom had said she looked pretty. Hana dabbed some on her lips but rubbed it off hastily. It was too fake. Okay then, what about eye stuff? She'd never tried any. What if it looked weird and she couldn't get it off?

The bathroom door, which was missing its lock,

opened as she was aiming the mascara brush at her lashes.

"Sorry, but I've gotta go," Elena said. She was still in her pink nightshirt. "What are you up to?" she asked.

"Umm. I was just—"

"Borrowing my makeup. I pay for that out of my own allowance, you know."

"I'll pay you back."

"No, that's okay. So long as you don't make a habit of it." Elena used the toilet and flushed it. Hana grimaced, wishing her sister was more modest about her bodily functions. "How come you're interested in your appearance all of a sudden?" Elena asked.

Hana fumbled for a safe excuse without finding one.

"Hana, are you getting interested in boys?" Elena asked suddenly.

"No."

"I bet you saw some cute guy on the beach. That's it, isn't it?"

"No."

Elena narrowed her eyes. "Oh, come on, Hana. I'm your big sister. You can tell me."

"Why? You never talk to me about your boyfriends." Hana was still hurt that Elena had not confided in her the night she came back crying after her last date with her boyfriend, Rob.

"That's because you're such a baby you wouldn't understand. In fact, I'm surprised you're even interested. . . . Have you seen someone you like, Hana?"

"No. I told you. No boys."

"Well, okay." Elena sighed. "Come on. I'll show you how to do your eyes right."

Hana stood still and let Elena make her up.

"There," Elena said. "Not too much. That'd be weird at your age, but just enough to give you some color—Hana, you look *great!* See?" Elena turned her around so she could face herself in the bathroom mirror.

Hana stared wide-eyed at her own image. She had become one of those expensive dolls with a porcelain face. Artificially pretty and just for show. "Uh uh," Hana said, reaching for the washcloth.

"Let Mom see." Elena pulled the washcloth away from Hana and started dragging her out of the bathroom. Hana clung to the sink. "See what I mean? You are *such* a baby," Elena said. She dropped Hana's arm and walked out in disgust.

Hana washed the makeup off. It wouldn't stay on when she went swimming anyway, she told herself.

"Oh, you!" Elena said when Hana got to the breakfast table, plain faced as ever.

Mom hugged Hana and told her older daughter, "Don't rush her. Hana can stay my baby as long as she likes."

Hana frowned and pulled away from her mother. "I'm not a baby. And not just because I don't like makeup," she said. "I'm going to read on the beach."

"Again? You practically live on that beach," Mom said. "We're going to Duck Harbor this morning. Your father wants to try the fishing there and the boys are coming. You come, too, Hana."

"Do I have to?"

"Why don't you want to be with your family? Didn't you have fun with Elena and me yesterday?" Mom sounded hurt.

"It's not that—" Hana grabbed the first excuse that came to mind. "It's that Duck Harbor's so rocky it hurts my feet to swim there."

"I told you I'd buy you a pair of those swim shoes," Mom said.

"Meanwhile, could I just go to my beach?"

"Your beach?" Mom questioned. But then she gave in. "Well, tell you what. We won't be ready for a while anyway, so you go and we'll pick you up when we're leaving."

Hana thanked her mother, grabbed her book, and escaped out the sliding door onto the back deck. As she shut the screen door behind her, she saw Elena studying her suspiciously, but she was so glad to be going to the beach that she didn't worry. She pulled a beach towel off the clothesline and ran.

The sun was bright. Two families had already staked out their spaces with beach umbrella, cooler, chairs, and sand toys. Hana settled on her rock, which was vacant for a change. She spread out her towel, crossed her legs under her, and checked casually to see if Mr. Crane was there. None of the nooks along the sea wall were occupied and nobody was in swimming yet.

What would they start off talking about if he did come along? She could tell him something else about his teaching. Something good. Maybe how much she'd appreciated the long messages he wrote on her papers. Most teachers didn't take the time to explain what they'd liked or how something a student had written could be improved. In fifth grade Mrs. Tracy hadn't even bothered to return half the papers the class wrote, and she never explained why she gave a mark.

Only, was it right to encourage him to go back to teaching? Maybe he'd be a lot better at rafting trips or playing the saxophone. She smiled, thinking of how he must look playing the sax with his cheeks puffed out and his eyes half closed. Did she dare to ask him if he'd brought his instrument along and if she could hear him play?

This time, she saw him arrive. He had stopped at the entrance to the beach between the sea walls and was looking around. He smiled when he spotted her on the rocks and came right toward her.

She was thrilled. "Hi, Mr. Crane," she said. "I was just going in for a swim."

"Go ahead. If it's not too cold, I'll follow you. And my name is David, remember?"

She nodded and said softly, "David." Then she climbed off the rocks and did a shallow dive into the greenish water. It was cold, but as usual, her body adjusted to it by the time she'd swum a few yards. When she turned around to see where Mr. Crane was, he was splashing along behind her.

"Race you to the next breakwater," he said. It wasn't more than sixty yards away.

He outdistanced her easily even though he swam awkwardly, but she came in not too far behind him.

"Did you learn to swim at this beach?" he asked, treading water and waiting for her.

"No, at the Y at home. Mom made us take every swim class they offered. She's afraid of the water and she wanted us to be good swimmers."

"Who's us?"

"My brothers. Eric's seventeen and Alan's almost sixteen. And then I have a sister, Elena, who's fifteen."

"Oh, right. I should have remembered. You wrote about them a lot, didn't you?" He was grinning, and she hoped he wasn't remembering that some of what she'd written was pretty critical. "You know," he said wistfully, "you're lucky to have brothers and sisters. I was an only child."

She wrinkled her nose. "But being the youngest is awful," she said. "I'd much rather be an only child."

"Why's that?" He realized how shallow the water was and put his feet down. Even she could stand, although the water came up to her neck.

"Because my parents won't believe I'm grown up," Hana said. "They're going to treat me like a baby my whole life."

He chuckled. "You sound so despairing."

"Well, it's pretty bad. Like back home, they don't go out unless they can find a baby sitter for me, but my sister Elena was baby sitting *me* when she was my age. It makes me mad."

"I can see it would. Especially since you're mature for your age."

"I am?"

"I think so. Anyway, I haven't met anyone your age I'm as comfortable talking to."

The compliment tasted like melted chocolate to her. "Thank you," she said gratefully.

They were drying off on the rocks and talking about which frozen yogurt tasted as good as ice cream—a subject Hana had neglected to consider in her list of conversational material—when she saw Elena on the beach. Elena stopped short and stared at Hana and Mr. Crane.

"Uh oh," Hana said. "Here's my sister."

"The fifteen-year-old? She looks a lot older."

"That's because her body developed so early," Hana said matter-of-factly. She was aghast to see Mr. Crane blush.

Elena had finally walked the rest of the way to the rocks.

"Hi," she said.

"Hi," Mr. Crane replied, none too brilliantly, Hana thought. She didn't like the abashed way he was smiling at Elena either. "Are you an advocate of Cherry Garcia frozen yogurt like your sister?"

"I like any kind," Elena said. "Hana's the fussy one. She'll only eat frozen yogurt with fruit."

"I'm partial to chocolate myself. You know there are studies that claim it really does make you happy? . . . I'm David Crane." He held out his hand. "Hana's sixth-grade English teacher?"

"And she met you on the beach today?" Elena asked.

"Yesterday . . . I'm here for a week."

"Alone?"

"All by my lonesome."

"It's a funny place to come by yourself," Elena said. "Mostly it's families around here." She perched somewhat gingerly on the crest of a tilted rock next to them.

"Oh, I know Wellfleet. My family brought me here a decade ago, when I was Hana's age. I remember there used to be square dances on the pier."

"They still have them Wednesday nights," Elena said.

"And do you girls go?"

"Usually," Elena said.

"I hated them when I was a kid," he said. "My mother used to make me dance with her because my father didn't dance, and I felt ridiculous."

"Maybe we'll go tonight," Elena said. "I think my mother said something about going."

"Well, since my mother's not here, I may give it another try," he said.

Hana watched him chatting easily with Elena. She felt herself receding from them, until she'd gone clear out of the conversational space—until she was alone the way she so often was with her family.

A black Lab crossed the beach unattended.

"That's what I like about Wellfleet," Mr. Crane said to Elena. "It doesn't change. People still ignore the NO DOGS ON THE BEACH sign as if they can't read."

"That dog belongs to the man who owns the cottages behind the sea wall," Elena said. "It thinks it owns the beach." She turned to Hana and asked, "Remember when you used to be afraid of dogs?"

"I'm not anymore," Hana said hurriedly for Mr. Crane's benefit.

"I guess not. You also used to be too shy to talk much. Looks like that's changed, too." Elena studied her speculatively. "Well, so are you coming to Duck Harbor with us? Mom sent me to get you."

Hana considered. She certainly didn't want Elena telling the family that she was staying on the beach with her English teacher. Who knew what they'd make of that? "Okay," she said, and stood up. "I'm coming."

"I guess we'll see you at the square dance tonight then, Mr. Crane," Elena said in parting.

"I'll look for you," he said. "If you girls will dance with me, it might even be fun."

They waved at him and ran off the beach together. She'd wear her swing skirt, Hana decided, and maybe even some lipstick.

"Well, how about you!" Elena said when they were out of earshot of the beach and had slowed down.

"How about me what?"

"I figured you'd found a boy. But a grown man!"

"He was my teacher."

"Yeah, but he's young."

"Not that young. He finished college."

"Umm," Elena said. "Well, you just better watch it, Hana. You never know."

"You never know what?"

"How some guys are."

"Mr. Crane just likes to talk to me," Hana said in outrage at her sister's insinuation.

"Fine. I just said to be careful. Are you going to tell Mom?"

"Tell Mom what?"

"That you met your teacher on the beach."

"I already told her that."

"You did?" Elena seemed surprised. "She didn't say anything to me."

"Because she didn't make a big deal of it, like you are," Hana said.

"Wow, aren't we touchy!" Elena had a smirk on her face that Hana wished she could wipe off.

Chapter 5

Hana's cotton swing skirt brushed lightly as butterfly wings against her sun-warmed skin as she whirled joyously around the deck. She had been the first one dressed for the square dance and now she was waiting. Elena had lent her a scoop neck T-shirt that had shrunk drastically the first time it went through the wash. It didn't scoop much on Hana, but it went well with the flowered swing skirt. Elena had also lent her a fancy clip to hold her hair back in place of the usual rubber band.

"Want me to make up your eyes for you?" Elena asked from the other side of the screen door. "I'll do it so that Mom won't even notice."

Hana hesitated, then she nodded and sat patiently at the glass umbrella table while Elena worked on her.

"You look good," Elena said when she'd finished.

"Too bad he won't be able to see you that well in the dark."

"He may not even come. I bet he doesn't. He's probably forgotten all about the dance."

"What's he doing here alone, anyway? He must be kind of strange."

"No, Elena. He needs to think about his future."

"I thought he had a future. He's a teacher."

"Well, he thinks maybe he'd be better off doing something else."

"He talked to you about his career?" Elena sounded impressed.

"He talked to me about his teaching because, after all, I *was* his student."

"Umm." Elena pinched Hana's cheek and advised, "Just remember you're still a little kid. You don't know how lucky you are not to have to think about some things, Hana."

"What things? I may be little, but I'm not a kid. Just because I don't say much doesn't mean I don't think."

Elena eyed her narrowly and didn't reply. It made Hana angry that Elena still wouldn't mention her boyfriend. She was always talking to Mom about him when she thought Hana wasn't listening.

Mom noticed the makeup immediately. "Hana! What are you all dolled up for?"

"The square dance," Elena said. "Her teacher said he'd be there."

"Oh." Mom smiled indulgently. "Well, you do look nice, baby. I hope he shows up. I can't remember which one he was. There were so many at that parent-teacher conference last spring."

"He was the one who told you I was a good student."

Mom laughed. "Of course you're a good student, Hana. You take school seriously, not like your brothers—or your big sister when she's got boy problems." Mom rolled her eyes pointedly at Elena.

"Mom, that's a rotten thing to say. Don't I always pass my courses?" Elena protested. "I'm not like Alan. When did you ever have to go to school for *me* because I was failing?"

"I didn't say you were a goof-off, Elena. But you do admit that this past year—"

"You always pick on me!" Elena cried. She ran back into the cottage. Mom sighed and followed after her, no doubt to apologize. If she didn't, Elena would sulk for the whole evening.

———

The square dance was held at the end of the long pier, past the harbormaster's house and past the lineup of expensive pleasure boats docked in high-priced slips. Cars were parked four deep at least three-quarters of the way down the wide pier.

As soon as Dad parked the van, Eric and Alan dashed off to their basketball game. "They could at least have waited to see if there was anyone in the crowd they wanted to dance with," Mom said.

"The boys have gotten too old for this kind of thing," Dad said.

"So have I, in case nobody's noticed," Elena said. "It's mostly preschoolers that come."

"Only the first hour or two," Mom said. "Then it's for adults."

"Not anymore. Now people take their five-year-olds as partners even though the little kids don't know what they're doing and mess up the patterns." Elena spoke from experience. "Don't expect me to dance in a square with any little kids."

"So why did you come?" Dad asked her.

"Tradition, I guess. And I'm sick of TV."

"Last year you met a boy at the dance," Hana reminded her.

"Yeah, and he wrote to me once, but I never got around to answering."

"Well, if he's here, you can apologize," Mom said. Her eyes were sparkling. What she loved about the Wellfleet square dances was that whole families attended from grandparents down to toddlers. "It's such a family thing," Mom had said more than once, giving it her stamp of approval.

The caller was organizing groups for the Virginia reel. That dance was the unofficial end of the little kids' part of the evening's program. Tall and thin, and sounding as New England as anyone could, the caller stood up on his high platform above the sound system and patiently directed the hundreds of would-be dancers. His mix of humor and authority got them moving in the right directions—mostly. People of all ages were dressed in shorts and baggy sweatshirts do-si-doing and galumphing around unselfconsciously. A burst of laughter usually meant someone had messed up the steps and was laughing at himself.

Hana backed away from the group her family had joined. Elena's partner was a young father whose wife was dancing with their kindergarten-age son, just as Elena had predicted. Mom offered to step out and let Hana dance with Dad, but Hana shook her head and kept going.

The last orange shred of sunset was disappearing into the darkness toward Chequesset Neck, and the tall overhead lights shed pale halos at regular inter- vals along the pier. Hana walked around the fringe of the crowd of nondancers looking for Mr. Crane— David. Looking for David. She would die if he didn't come. She would die if he did. What if he were already there dancing with someone else? More likely he was home reading and had forgotten to come. She didn't see him. She didn't see him anywhere.

Oh, yes, she did. There he was! He was being pulled into a rowdy group of people who were mostly his age. They were tugging each other about giddily, trying to teach one of their number the movements.

"Now you all know the Virginia reel, right?" the caller asked in his calm nasal voice.

"Right," the crowd assured him in a unified roar.

"Fine. Then we'll just start the music and you follow the calls."

Hana watched Mr. Crane dance the Virginia reel. His partner was a bouncy old lady in baggy jeans. He was a little clumsy, but willing, and he didn't seem to get embarrassed when he made a mistake. Hana hated making a mistake. It made her feel like a bug under a microscope, and afterward she would be certain no one really wanted to be partners with a girl as awkward as she.

As he was coming down the line and turning under the arch made by the arms of the head couple, David spotted her. He grinned and waved. She waved back with a slight lift of her hand and immediately dissolved into the crowd so that he wouldn't realize she'd been standing there watching him.

She found her family again and waited until they were on the last movement and had bowed to their corners and to their partners as the caller bid them do. They broke from the formality of their double line, smiling and a bit dazed.

"Where were you, Hana?" Mom asked. "I could easily have dropped out and let you dance with your father."

"I didn't want you to," Hana said. She waited until her mother was distracted by Dad, who was complaining that his shoe was pinching his sore big toe, before she slipped away again. Mr. Crane found her as she was making her way toward the stanchions on the outside edges of the wharf.

"Would you be my partner for the next dance, Miss Riley?" he asked with mock formality.

"Sure," she said. His question had knocked the breath out of her and that one word was all she could manage. He held out his hand. She put her hand in his and saw the night air shimmer around her from the magic of his touch.

Now the caller had them forming squares of eight. "Couple one is the pair of you with your backs to me," he explained. "Couple one raise your hands." Somehow Hana and David found themselves in a square with Elena, partnered with a boy her age who behaved like a jumping jack. Elena kept trying to distance herself from him as he flung out his arms and kicked up his legs.

First they had to walk through the dance, beginning with "Circle to the left around the ring." Elena was too distracted by her partner to pay much attention to her sister, for which Hana was grateful. She thought she was going to faint from the pleasure of holding David's bony fingers and feeling his arm across her back as he promenaded her around the ring.

"I kind of like square dancing," he said. "Too bad I never get to do it."

"I like it, too," Hana said. "But mostly I only get to do it here in Wellfleet on vacation."

"I suppose I should know your parents from parent-teacher conferences," David said apologetically, "but I'm afraid I've forgotten what they look like."

"They're here." Hana gestured over her shoulder. "Over in that square near the platform. And you met my sister Elena on the beach today. That's her."

"Oh, right. Hi, Elena." He waved across the square.

Elena didn't notice. Her partner was apologizing for kicking her and she was glaring at him.

"I'm terrible at names and faces," Mr. Crane said. "Another bad fault in a teacher."

"Did you decide yet, Mr.—David?"

"No, I'm still wrestling with it. Might need some more consultation on the beach tomorrow if you have the time."

"Oh, yes," she said.

They allemanded left and did a ladies' star and then a men's star. The first couple walked through their steps with each couple in the square and then the other couples took their turns. Whenever Hana returned to her partner, her heart floated up in her chest.

Smiling tenderly at her, David said, "You're looking very pretty tonight, Hana."

She bit her lip and stared up at him. Should she tell him he looked handsome? He did look good with his suntan and his white, open-collared shirt against his thin neck. He was as elegant and sharp-featured as a hawk. But she didn't dare say anything.

"Hana," Elena whispered to her during a ladies' chain. "Are you going to faint in his arms? He's too old for you. Stop acting like a jerk."

"I'm not."

"You should just see yourself—" They were whirled apart in the next movement.

Next time they got close, Hana had tears of embarrassment in her eyes from Elena's remark. Elena's own eyes registered surprise when she saw Hana's expression.

As soon as the dance ended, Mr. Crane said, "How about introducing me to your parents again, Hana?"

Subdued, Hana located her parents in one of the clumps of people chatting with one another between sets. Elena was already heading toward them. Hana followed, leading David. She was sure this meeting was going to embarrass her in some way, but he'd asked, so she had no choice.

David seemed comfortable with her parents, who behaved as they always did with teachers. Mom chirruped eagerly and Dad got solemn and grumpy. He had not, he'd once admitted, been a good student himself. David smiled politely at them and flattered them by saying how glad he was to have bumped into his favorite student on the beach.

"Do you come to Wellfleet often on vacation?"

"Not since my parents brought me when I was a kid, but I wanted a quiet place where I could think, and this fits the bill."

"You've got a lot to think about?" Dad asked in his brusque way.

"Uh huh—you know, career choices. Hana's been very helpful as a sounding board."

"Hana?" Dad examined her as if it startled him to imagine her being useful.

"Hana's a deep thinker," David said.

Dad's eyebrows went up and he cleared his throat

at length. Then he said, "Well, we better get in line before they close the ice cream stand."

"Mind if I join you?" David asked.

"Oh, do," Mom said. "I want to hear more about Hana's schoolwork. She never had a teacher who seemed so impressed with her before."

"Well, I admire originality, and Hana's writing was fresh and original," David said.

"You don't say!" Now it was Mom's turn to sound surprised.

David walked with them the length of the pier, ignoring Hana, to her dismay, and chatting away about the Wellfleet commercial shellfishing industry. Dad's contribution was to grunt now and then. Mom's was to pretend interest. Hana was forced to trail behind the three adults with Elena. She would have felt left out except that Elena kept poking her and chuckling as if Hana were the best of jokes.

"Cut it out," Hana said.

"Oh, you're so cool!" Elena teased. "I can't get over it, you and a teacher."

"Elena, please!" Hana begged, and for a few minutes Elena let her be.

At the ice cream stand Dad paid for everyone, and when David tried to give him the money for his cone, Dad refused to take it.

"Thanks," David said. "Next time I'll treat."

"You're going to be here next Wednesday?" Dad asked.

Sheepishly, David admitted he was only there for the week. Hana glared at her father for embarrassing her teacher by showing his offer to be an empty gesture.

The five of them stood in a loose circle, busily licking away at the cones before the ice cream could drip down onto their clothes.

"Nice moon tonight," Mom said.

"Should be a good day for fishing tomorrow. You fish?" Dad asked David.

"No, I don't," David admitted.

"Vergil's main interest in Wellfleet is the fishing," Mom said.

"It's not much good anymore. The place is fished out," Dad said.

"There's a lot here to enjoy, though," David said.

"Do you sail?" Elena asked.

"No. About all I do is swim and read."

"Sounds like Hana," Elena said.

Everyone looked at Hana, who had retreated into silence. She squirmed under their scrutiny and was relieved when they finally finished their cones and said good night. The Rileys walked back down the pier to their van. Eric and Alan were already dozing in the back of it.

"He's certainly a nice young man," Mom said about David Crane.

"And he really likes Hana," Elena said pointedly.

"Well, why shouldn't he?" Mom asked.

"No reason," Elena said. "But she *is* a little girl."

"Oh, Elena!" Mom's tone dismissed Elena's insinuation.

Hana shut her ears. It had been the most exciting evening of her life, preceded by the most wonderful afternoon, and she didn't want it ruined by her sister or anyone else. She watched the moon follow them home like a loving pet and thought about seeing David tomorrow. She hoped if he consulted with her as he'd promised that she would say the right thing. Something profound. Something wise. Something to prove she wasn't a little kid like her family thought.

Chapter 6

The rain had made a puddle on the windowsill and was dripping onto Hana's quilt when she woke up. She stood on the bed to slide the window shut. Elena was still asleep, curled around her pillow in the bed nearest the door.

No beach today if this rain keeps up, Hana thought with dismay. In a gentle drizzle, it was fun to put on Grandma's yellow slicker and trace the edge of the waves barefooted. Other people would be out poking at shells and crabs and seaweed. But in this heavy a rain, even the most avid beach walker stayed home. And so would David.

Maybe it would stop. On the Cape, Dad always said, "Wait a minute and the weather'll change." Right now David might be opening his eyes to the rain and closing them to go back to sleep. What would she do if it rained all day? Read, as usual, or maybe work on a jigsaw puzzle with Mom.

On rainy days, Alan's favorite activity was to bake a cake with decorative frosting so fancy it looked like a bakery-made cake. But he chased everyone from the kitchen when he worked. Did David have a hobby like that? She could ask him. If she saw him. If he hadn't gotten disgusted with the weather and left Wellfleet already.

The rain had curled her hair, Hana noticed in the mirror as she brushed her teeth. The straight brown ends were turned up, and tendrils of hair corkscrewed prettily around her forehead. This was as good as she ever looked. If only David could see her now!

Eric volunteered to make omelets in the kitchen. Omelets were his specialty. Hana asked for one with cheese and bacon bits. He looked disgusted and asked, "How about cheese and salsa?"

"I like bacon bits even if they're fake, Eric." Her brother liked his food pure and preferably vegetarian.

"You add them at the end yourself, then," he said.

Mom and Dad had already eaten.

"I'm going to fix that faucet in the basement bathroom," Dad said, and he grumbled, "Place is rusting away to nothing in this sea air you all like so much." He disappeared down the basement stairs.

Mom was still in her housecoat doing a crossword

puzzle from last Sunday's newspaper. "I like rainy days," she said. "It's so cozy in here."

Hana ate her cheese omelet with bacon bits sprinkled on top. She thanked Eric and folded herself into the biggest armchair with one of her books, but instead of reading she sat there imagining what David was doing. Did he cook for himself? Thin as he was, he probably didn't eat much. A bagel or sweet roll for breakfast. Yes. And then? Maybe he was busy making a list of the good and bad things about going back for another year of teaching. Only she doubted that he was a list maker. Impulsive decisions would be more his style.

She might have been wrong to encourage him to think he was a good teacher. Every teacher Hana had ever had could at least keep order in the classroom— all except David. Would he be able to learn? Mom and Dad believed you could learn how to do anything. Hana wasn't so sure. Becoming a disciplinarian when he wasn't one naturally would mean changing his very nature, she suspected. And she liked David Crane just the way he was.

Alan had taken over the kitchen now and was frosting a cake. She wondered when he'd had a chance to bake it. Probably before she woke up. He usually ran early in the morning and he wouldn't have been able to today. Alan always had to be doing something.

The rain hammered away at the roof and streamed down the windows, effectively wrapping the family up inside the cottage. Eric emerged from the bathroom he'd been hogging for a while. He spotted Alan's cake and asked, "Is that for looking at or eating?"

"Eating. After dinner tonight," Alan said.

"Why can't I have a piece now?"

"Because you'll ruin it."

"Are you going to eat any of it, Alan?" Mom asked over her shoulder.

"I can't. Making these things takes my appetite away."

"So what did you do, spit in the batter or something?" Eric asked.

"Not a bad idea. Wish I'd thought of it," Alan said. He finished a raspberry-colored rose with a flourish and tossed the decorating tube at the sink piled high with dirty dishes. "There. Keep away from my cake or else, Eric," Alan warned. He ran downstairs where they could hear Dad banging at something metallic.

"What do you suppose he's up to now?" Eric asked Mom.

"Who knows? Alan's always up to something,"

Mom said as she erased a word and turned to consult the dictionary flipped open at her elbow.

Elena sauntered into the living room with her manicure box, having just gotten out of bed. "Hi," she said. "What a rotten day, huh?"

"Your grandmother's petunias need the rain. This saves our having to water them," Mom said. "Are you going to eat breakfast, Elena?"

"It's too late. I'll wait for lunch." She settled onto the couch with her manicure box, propping one bare foot on top of the coffee table so she could work on her toes comfortably.

A minute later, Alan barged into the living room.

"Mom, how about telling Dad to give me the car for a couple of hours? He says one of you might want to go somewhere. But you're all just lying around and I've got to get together with a guy in P-Town."

Mom answered without lifting her eyes from her puzzle. "Can't you do it tomorrow, Alan? I don't like you driving on wet roads. Anyway, Eric would have to go with you. You just have your learner's permit, after all."

"Nobody in this family gives me a break," Alan complained. "I'll go stir crazy stuck in this cottage all day."

"You could *bike* down to P-Town," Eric said.

"Twelve miles in the rain?"

Mom rose and stretched. Glancing over the counter into the kitchen, she said, "Look at that mess! Who's going to clean up? Not me, I'll tell you."

"I made breakfast. Cooks don't do dishes," Eric said. "Besides, Alan made the worst mess with his frosting."

"Is that all the thanks I get?" Alan bellowed. He marched into the kitchen and picked up the cake he'd just finished. "Might as well throw this in the garbage then," he said.

"Alan! Stop acting crazy and put that cake down," Mom said.

Alan lowered the cake to the counter. Sullenly he asked, "How about Elena? Why don't you get her to stop primping and do something useful for a change?"

Elena was painting her toenails blue and gold. "I didn't even eat breakfast. Why should I have to clean up?"

"Fine, then let Hana do it," Alan said, and he whirled off to the room he shared with Eric, slamming the door.

Mom eyed Hana. "You know," she said, "it wouldn't hurt you to straighten up the kitchen. It's better than ruining your eyes reading all day."

Hana rinsed the plates the way Mom wanted because she claimed Grandma's dishwasher didn't do dirty dishes well. Then she stacked the dishes in the dishwasher and started on the pans. How could those boys have dirtied so many pans and mixing bowls for a couple of omelets and a cake?

The rain was coming down less forcefully now. Probably David was on the beach and she'd miss him while she scoured pots like Cinderella. That's what she was in this family: Cinderella. Tears smarted as she rubbed at the burned spots on the cake pan. Alan was so mean and Eric wasn't much better. She hated her brothers. If they weren't treating her like a baby, they were sticking her with rotten jobs.

Elena was leaning against the kitchen doorway waving her fingers in the air. "I'd dry, but it would smudge my nails. . . . You chasing off to the beach after your teacher when you're done?"

"So what if I am?"

"It's sick, Hana. Honestly, he's way too old for you."

Mom came into the kitchen, picked up a dish-towel, and began drying the clean bowls Hana had stacked in the draining rack. "What are you girls talking about?"

"Hana's teacher, Mr. Crane," Elena said.

"The young man at the square dance? He seemed

like a nice fellow. I think he was embarrassed when your father wouldn't let him pay for his own cone."

"Sure he was embarrassed," Elena said. "Daddy treats everybody like a little kid. But don't you think—"

"Elena, can't you mind your own business?" Hana asked.

As soon as the kitchen was back in order, Hana pulled Grandma's yellow slicker off the peg behind the door. The slicker was man-sized and came to her ankles, but she loved it. She rolled up the sleeves and had her hand on the door when Eric appeared behind her.

"Hey, I'm using that," he said. "It's too big for you anyway, squirt." And he pulled it off her shoulders.

"I had it first!" Hana said.

"Yeah, but you don't count." He leaned back toward the living room to say, "I'm biking into Wellfleet, Mom."

"What for?" she asked. But he was gone.

Hana decided to go to the beach anyway. So what if she got wet? She opened the door.

"Hana," Mom said. "You're not going out in this rain."

"What's the difference whether I'm walking in the rain or going swimming, Mom? You get wet both ways."

"Don't you talk back to me, Hana. I get enough of that from your brothers." Mom sounded upset. "A little rain makes everybody so crabby," she complained, and went back to her puzzle.

David wasn't there, of course. Had she really expected that a person who had a car would be walking on the wet beach in a drizzle? He had probably driven to Provincetown to cruise the shops and stare at the other people. That was what everyone did when it rained. Except her family, because they hated the heavy traffic and not being able to find a parking space. She should have worn something over her T-shirt. She was cold as well as wet and it was raining hard enough again for the water to blur her vision and drip off the end of her nose.

A herring gull ambled over to Hana hoping for a handout, all the while looking the other way and pretending it wasn't.

"Sorry, I don't have anything for you," she said.

The sleek, white bird had its neat, gray wings folded against its sides like a pair of umbrellas. Immune to the rain, it sidled past her as if that had been its intention all along.

What if David really had left the Cape and she never had a chance to talk to him again? Because in the fall she'd be in middle school, and even if he went back to teaching, he'd be in a different building. She could go see him, the way kids went back to see their favorite teachers, but then what would they say to each other? Standard things. How do you like seventh grade? Fine. How do you like teaching this year, Mr. Crane. Fine. And there would be other people around to remind them that she was the student and he was the teacher. He wouldn't be confiding his secret doubts to her. She'd have lost the status of mature person that he'd granted her this summer.

By the time she got back to the cottage, she was shivering so hard from being wet and cold that Mom got upset and made her take a hot shower and put on a sweatshirt and dry jeans.

"If you don't catch pneumonia, it'll be a miracle," Mom said. It was what she always said when one of her children came home drenched, even though none of them had ever had pneumonia.

The rest of the afternoon Hana spent curled up in a chair, reading and quietly mourning David Crane. He had waved his magic wand and transformed her into a person whose opinions and judgments were worth listening to, but that brief transformation was over. Now she was back in Cinderella's rags again . . . and all because of a rainy day. Bad luck, bad luck, bad luck, she thought bitterly.

Chapter 7

The cottage was fogged-in Friday morning. Hana could barely see past Dad's van to the sand lane when she looked out her window into the spongy gray mist. She sighed. Another lost day, and there were no more left. Even if David hadn't left Wellfleet yesterday, he was due to go tomorrow. Week-long rentals only went from Saturday to Saturday.

She moped her way through a bowl of cereal and a glass of orange juice, ignoring the bickering between Elena and Eric over who should get the last egg in the refrigerator. Finally Mom told Eric to get in the car and go to Cumberland Farms for eggs and milk.

"Your father and I are shopping for your cousin's wedding present in Hyannis today," she said. "Who'd like to come with us?"

"Me," Elena said. "I need some things."

"What things?" Mom asked. "We shopped for you in Orleans, Elena."

"Just stuff, Mom, nail polish and like that," Elena said. "Nothing I can't pay for out of my allowance."

"Well, get ready then. If we're going to beat the traffic, we have to start in an hour. And you had best come with us, too, Hana."

"No, Mom! I hate shopping."

"I'm not leaving you alone for the whole day."

"Eric and Alan will be here. Besides, I'm plenty old enough to stay alone."

Mom considered. "Well, we'll see what Eric says when he gets back with the eggs."

In despair, Hana rushed off to check out the beach before her fate could be decided. Tears mixed with the cool damp of the fog as she stared at the foamy edge of the water. It lapped over the sand like the top of a sheet over a comforter.

"Hey, Hana," a voice called. "What are you doing up so early on this foggy morning?"

Her whole body went rigid with joy. "Mr. Crane!"

He grinned. "So one day of not seeing me and we're back to formal address, are we?"

"Oh, I mean—"

"I'm just kidding you. Mr. Crane is fine if you're

more comfortable with it. My problem is I still think of myself as a college kid. 'Mister' makes me feel like an impostor."

"I'm sorry."

He dismissed her embarrassment with a smile. "How many books did you read yesterday?"

"Just one."

"What was it?"

"Some old mystery my grandma had in the cottage. The whole last chapter was missing."

He laughed. "Perfect excuse for a writing exercise. If we were in class, I'd make you write your own ending."

She was finally relaxing enough to smile at him. "You were always good at making us want to write things."

"Yeah," he said. "I was good at some things to do with teaching, wasn't I? While I gnaw away at my faults, I forget that . . . I still haven't decided what to do."

"Did *you* read a lot of books yesterday?"

"No, I brooded. I'm a great brooder. But today I woke up feeling better. Listen, the weatherman claims this fog is going to lift. Want to go on a whale watch with me?"

"Oh, I'd love to," she said. "Last year my family went, but I had a cold so Mom made me stay home with my sister. Elena can't go on a boat. She gets seasick."

"You mean you've never been on a whale watch?"

"A couple of times when I was young."

He laughed. "Are you old now?"

"No, but I'm not a little kid anymore."

"True, you're not. In fact, you're very mature for your age, Hana." He said it sincerely. "Well, let's go ask your mother if it's okay."

"You want to go whale watching right now?"

"Yes, in time to make the eleven o'clock trip. The weather should be lifting by then, and if we're lucky nobody else will listen to the weather report and we'll have the boat to ourselves."

She shivered with delight at the idea of being alone with him, or nearly so, and promptly led him back to her grandmother's cottage, confident that her parents would still be waiting for Elena to get ready for their shopping trip.

The cottage was hidden from the road behind a thick growth of scrub oak and autumn olive and pitch pine. "Nice," David said when Hana had threaded him through the path Dad had made in the underbrush to the back deck. There a jaunty umbrella table and lounge chairs awaited use in better weather.

"I love this cottage," Hana said simply. "We come here every summer."

They entered the living room through the sliding glass door. Alan was stretched across the middle of the floor in his running outfit doing sit-ups in front of the TV. Mom was visible in the kitchen over the countertop that divided it from the living room. She was tasting the summer vegetable soup she'd already prepared for dinner.

"Hello there," Mom said. "How are you managing in this weather, Mr. Crane?"

"Oh, I don't mind weather," he said. "Some rain and fog is part of the Cape's charm. Anyway, it's supposed to clear up this afternoon and I'd like to go whale watching. Mind if I take Hana with me?"

"Mind? No. That's very kind of you to offer," Mom said. She hesitated, then she added, "But let me just ask my husband what he thinks."

"I'd be happy to take along any other family member who feels like coming," David said. "They say the whales are very active this year."

"So I've heard," Mom said. She fitted the cover back on the soup pot and went downstairs to the basement.

"I'm Alan," Alan said from the floor without stopping his sit-ups.

"The big brother," David said. "The one who makes models?"

"No, that's my brother, Eric. How did you know about that?"

"Hana often used her family for composition topics."

"No kidding?" Alan sat up and stayed up, braced against his hands. "What did she say about me?"

Hana sucked in her breath, hoping David wouldn't give her away. David glanced at her as he said, "—I don't actually remember much of what she wrote, just a few things. I was into model building, too, so that one stuck in my mind."

"She tell you about the time I sold one of Eric's World War II battleships to a kid because I needed the cash for a date?"

She had written that incident up and described how Eric got revenge by burying Alan's basketball in the woods and refusing to tell him where to find it.

Mom reappeared. "Vergil says it's fine with him if one of our other children goes with you, too." She looked a bit embarrassed, but she didn't explain why a sibling chaperone was being required.

"How about it, Alan? Want to go to P-Town with us?" David asked.

"Sure." Alan rose to his feet in one smooth movement. "We leaving right now?"

Hana couldn't believe it. Eric might have agreed to go, since he had an interest in animals and the environment, but Alan's interests mostly revolved around sports, fast-moving vehicles, and girls.

Mom insisted on making sandwiches for them, even though David said he would buy lunch for the three of them on the boat. Then, while David was using the bathroom, she gave Hana and Alan fifteen dollars each and privately instructed them to pay their own way. "Young teachers don't earn much," she said.

"Take a sweater or jacket," she advised as they were about to leave. "It can get cold on the water." And she waved them off with a worried, "I hope the fog does lift for you."

They were on the short sand driveway when suddenly Dad's head poked up above the stairs in the outside basement stairwell. "What kind of car do you drive, Mr. Crane?" Dad called.

"It's a Toyota Corolla, old but it gets regular servicing," David said. "Don't worry, Mr. Riley. I'm a cautious driver."

"Yeah," Dad said. "Lot of traffic to P-Town on a day like this. Better take your time."

Alan groused about his parents as they walked to David's rented room, which was over a garage a quarter of a mile down the road. "Can you believe them? You'd think they came straight out of the Dark Ages."

"Well, they've got a big investment of love and

years of caring in you guys. You should hear my mother, and I'm over twenty-one."

"You're what, twenty-two or -three?" Alan asked.

"Twenty-three—almost."

"Boy, I can't wait until I'm old enough to do as I please."

"I don't know if anybody ever gets *that* old," David said wryly.

"You sound like a teacher," Alan said.

"Sorry about that," David said. He turned to Hana, who was a step behind them. "You planning on remaining mute the rest of the day?"

"No," she said.

"Well, say something. Think this fog's going to lift?"

"Yes," she said.

"No opinions on the weather you want to express?"

"No," she said. The teasing had been so gentle that she didn't mind when both David and Alan laughed.

Hana was assigned to sit in the back seat of the Toyota. It was impressively messy, she thought. Dirty white socks littered the floor among papers and magazines—poetry and short story journals and *The Atlantic Monthly*. A travel magazine featuring Nepal lay face up on top.

In the front seat Alan was describing the kind of car he was going to buy. ". . . When I get the bucks, something low and fast like a Corvette. Meanwhile, I'm into motorcycles," he said. "This guy in P-Town does amazing things restoring old Harleys. He works out of this garage in the East End, and anybody who's interested can walk right in and be part of the action."

"Hmm," David said.

"You're not into motorcycles?"

"Not especially."

"Mind if I put on some music?" Alan asked.

For the rest of the half-hour trip, he blasted the air with heavy-duty rock loud enough to hurt Hana's ears. She plugged them with her fingers and wondered why David didn't ask Alan to turn down the volume. After all, it was David's radio.

As soon as they'd parked in a whale-watching car lot, Alan got out and said, "Thanks for the ride. I'll meet you guys here around three. That's when the eleven o'clock boat should get back, between two and three."

"You're not going with us?" David asked in surprise.

"No, I told you there's this guy—"

"But don't your folks expect—"

"Oh, come on, David. You don't need me to monitor you and my baby sister, do you?"

"That isn't the point," David said patiently. "Your parents expect—"

"Yeah, well, I didn't sign any contract. See you later." And Alan took off.

David turned to Hana. "That's why I didn't want to try teaching high school English. Guys like your brother can run right over me."

"Alan runs over everybody," Hana said.

Secretly, she was thrilled to be alone with him.

"Come on, then," he said. "Let's get our tickets."

The boat was fuller than he'd predicted. On the Cape, even vacationers listened to weather reports, apparently. The sun came out as the sturdy hundred-and-fifty-foot boat rounded the point past the final lighthouse and headed for Stellwagen Bank and the open sea. It couldn't have been a more perfect afternoon. Clean-laundered air and a gentle three-foot swell lulled them into tranquillity.

Hana and David had found seats on the top deck, halfway down the last row of benches that were open to the sky. They were surrounded by families with little kids, and for a while they watched three kindergarten-age boys showing off their belly buttons to one another.

"I like kids so long as they're someone else's responsibility," David said.

"Little kids are cute," Hana said, and hoped he wasn't thinking that she was little herself.

Two hours out of the harbor, they spotted the first whales spouting. The boat's lecturer had just finished describing the rescue of a whale tangled in fishermen's netting and how the animal had cooperated with the research team by holding still so they could cut it loose.

Hana squealed joyously as a baby whale jumped out of the water beside its mother. David was as exuberant as she. The baby flapped its tail playfully before diving in synchronization with its mother, who showed her white underside, sleek as a billowing sail, before she dove out of sight. It was a great day for whales, as the lecturer kept assuring them, in case they didn't realize how privileged they were. There were nearly a dozen whales to be seen performing all around the boat. People ran from port to starboard as whales breached and flapped their tails and spouted. One came up ten feet from where Hana was standing against the railing, rolled in the water, and fixed its eye on her as if it were curious about what manner of creature she might be. Even the most blasé passenger exclaimed in amazement at that.

"It was just fabulous!" Hana said, after the boat had turned and left the whales behind to make its way back to Provincetown.

"The best I've ever seen," David said. "You must be lucky for me, Hana."

"Did you decide yet?"

"What to do about teaching?"

She nodded.

"Well, I'm feeling more confident, more like I could go back and succeed this time out. But I don't know for sure yet. Would you think I was a coward if I didn't go back?"

"Oh, no." She couldn't imagine anything negative about him.

"So here's your English assignment for today." He put on a teacherly voice. "Describe this experience in one word."

"Awesome," she said without hesitation.

He laughed. "It was, wasn't it?"

Alan was leaning against the Toyota Corolla when they got back to it.

"Find the guy you were looking for?" David asked him.

Alan shrugged.

"Something go wrong?" David asked sympathetically.

Alan shook his head. He was in one of his black moods and he didn't talk on the way home, which Hana knew meant something hadn't worked out for him.

"Tomorrow's Saturday," Hana said. "Are you going to leave in the morning, David?"

"Unfortunately, yes."

"I guess you'll be leaving early," Hana said.

"Pretty early."

Hana sat quietly the rest of the way home. She was telling herself how stupid it was to be depressed because something was going to happen when it hadn't happened yet. She was wasting her last good moments with David by mourning the loss of him in advance. But no matter how she scolded herself for it, Hana couldn't stop feeling bad. David was out of her life tomorrow morning and she would be Cinderella again the minute he left.

Chapter 8

The family had just finished their soup that evening when Elena said, "Look at you smiling all over your face, Hana! That must have been some whale-watching trip."

"I saw a lot of whales," Hana said.

"I didn't know you were that interested in whales, Hana," Mom said as she calmly dished out the pasta primavera.

"It's Mr. Crane who interests her," Elena said.

"Don't give your little sister any ideas," Dad said. He had brought his tackle box to the table and was poking through the lures in preparation for his evening's fishing.

"Lots of kids get crushes on their teachers, Dad," Elena said. "But I never have, so she can't be learning it from me."

"Learning what?" Mom asked with a frown.

"Learning to think of teachers romantically," Elena said.

Leaving her serving spoon suspended in midair, Mom directed the frown at Hana. "You do look flushed. Are you feeling all right?"

"I'm fine," Hana said.

"Actually, she looks pretty," Eric put in. He had shaken half the jar of Parmesan onto his pasta.

"You do, Hana," Mom agreed as she resumed serving. "Are you wearing makeup?"

"No," Hana said.

Elena was laughing. "Mom, don't you understand what she's glowing about? She's in love. That's the look of love on your baby girl's face."

Hana pushed her dinner plate away from her. "Why do I always have to be the one that gets picked on in this family?" she asked.

"We're not picking on you," Eric said. "Didn't you hear me say you look pretty? That was a compliment, in case you didn't know."

"I don't care. I just wish you'd all leave me alone." Hana was trembling. She felt as if they were sniffing around her like predators after their prey.

"What did you and Mr. Crane talk about on the whale watch?" Mom asked.

"I don't know," Hana said. "Everything."

"What do you mean, *everything?*" Mom put an emphasis on the word that made it sound sinister.

"Just that David listens to me as if—like I might have an idea in my head."

"Not like you're a stupid little kid, you mean," Eric said.

"But she *is* a stupid little kid," Alan said. He had finished his pasta and was scraping what was left out of the pot.

Hana glared at him. Instead of being so nasty, he should be grateful that she hadn't given him away. Mom and Dad still didn't know that Alan hadn't even been on the whale watch with her.

"So what did *you* do while the whales were showing off, Alan?" Eric asked.

"What do you mean?"

"I'm just curious about your sudden interest in wild animals."

"Ah, shove it, Eric." Alan took the empty pot and his dish to the sink.

"My bet is, you were busy girl watching while your baby sister was making up to her teacher."

"Eric!" Mom said. "That's disgusting."

"I wasn't even on that boat," Alan burst out. "I changed my mind about going. There happened to be a motorcycle I wanted to see."

"You didn't stay with Hana?" Dad rumbled, putting aside his lures.

"Listen, Dad. Dave's a perfectly nice guy," Alan said. "He's not going to molest your baby girl on a *whale*-watching boat."

"That's not the point," Dad said. "Your mother thought Hana was with you, and now we find out— You're irresponsible, Alan. . . . And where's the money your mother gave you for the ticket?"

Alan shrugged. "I spent it."

"That does it. You're grounded until further notice," Dad roared. He slammed his tackle box shut and stomped to the front door.

"Vergil, what about your dessert?" Mom asked.

"I'll have it later," he said, and was gone.

"I hate this family," Alan yelled over his shoulder as he smacked the back door shut behind him on his way out to the deck.

"So what did happen on the boat—alone with David?" Elena asked Hana while Mom chased to the back deck after Alan and Eric got up to do the dishes. It was his night.

"We watched whales and talked."

"He didn't put his arm around you or kiss you? Come on, you can tell me."

"Oh, Elena!" Mom said in distress. She'd returned to the table in time to overhear her eldest daughter.

"Well, did he?" Elena asked Hana.

"It's none of anybody's business," Hana cried. "I had the best time of my life. Why do you have to ruin it?" She rushed out the front door, past Dad, who had bent over to retrieve his fishing rod from the back of the station wagon. He didn't even notice her.

David might be on Grandma's beach right now, waiting for the sunset, Hana thought. But that's where Dad had said he was planning to fish tonight, so she couldn't go there. Besides, even if Dad wasn't going to be on the beach, she couldn't speak to David now. Her feelings were in such a wild snarl that anything might fly out of her mouth. Even, "I love you, David. I will always love you. I'd rather be with you than my family. Take me away from them, please." How devastating to blurt out something like that and see him back off in shock. Anyway, she wasn't sure that she really did love him. And what if he didn't back off? No way could she handle that— it would be too awkward and scary. Imagining was one thing, but doing—doing was for when she was older.

Hana bypassed Grandma's patch of sand and ran a half mile down the road along the cove to the main public beach. The long breakwater at the end of it jutted out like a finger pointing the way to ships going in or out of Wellfleet's inner harbor. Nobody was fishing from those rocks this evening. She leapt from boulder to boulder out to the beacon light at the end and hid herself on the far side of its massive concrete base. Squatting there like a human barnacle, she couldn't be seen from shore.

Her thoughts circled back to David. He was an adult. Would he be shocked if she told him she loved him? No doubt the first thing he would say was that she was too young. But if she was, why was she suffering a yearning that felt worse than an earache? Surely something so powerful must be love. And the hurt wasn't just that he probably didn't love her back, but that he was leaving and she'd never have a chance to be close to him again. Who would she talk to? Who would understand? Not her family, not even her friends. The only one who understood her, who heard her and took her seriously, was David. She wished she knew what she could do about it. She wished she knew a way to hang on to him.

The sun slid into the sea without any flaming ribbons of orange or purple to celebrate its passing. Hana had worn herself out, thinking about what she should do that wouldn't be stupid and ruin David's favorable impression of her. Did she dare do anything? She couldn't remember ever being this upset.

Finally, she grew weary of thinking and picked her way across the rocks where a lone fisherman was now sending his line zinging out into the dark water. The moon had come up and the night was bright with its light.

Nobody was home but Elena when Hana dragged in.

"Oh, boy, are you in trouble!" Elena said.

"Me? What did I do?"

"The way you ran out without eating anything . . . Mom got upset and she sent Eric and me looking for you. Where were you, anyway?"

"On the breakwater by the harbor."

"No, you weren't. I walked that far and I didn't see you."

"Well, I was there."

"Anyway, Mom decided maybe you went to Mr. Crane's, so she made Alan show her where he's staying and she paid him a visit."

"She didn't! What happened?"

"I don't know. She's not back yet."

Hana glared at her sister. "Elena, why do you always have to start something? I don't do anything to you, and you always try to get me in trouble."

"I do not."

"Yes, you do. You were the one who made it sound nasty, just because I had a good time."

"You make me out so mean," Elena said, as if Hana had shocked her.

"You *are* mean to me."

Elena turned her head away and didn't say a word. That could be denial or it could be that she was actually considering what Hana had said. Either way, Elena wasn't Hana's main concern.

Hana drank a glass of water and waited. The longer she waited, the more anxious she got about what her mother could be saying to Mr. Crane. Half an hour later, when her mother returned, Hana felt sick to her stomach.

"Where were you?" Mom asked.

"On the rocks. Elena didn't go far enough to see me. But I was there. . . . What did you say to Mr. Crane, Mom?"

"Nothing much. We just had a little talk."

"Mom, what did you say to him? I couldn't stand it if you made him feel bad when he didn't do anything but be nice to me." Hana was trembling again.

"Hana," Mom chided. "There's nothing to be so upset about. I told him that I didn't think it was a good idea for him to continue this relationship with you, that's all. I said you were making too much out of it."

"Oh, no! Mom, how could you do that to me? What do you think was going to happen? He's leaving tomorrow morning."

"I don't want *anything* to happen," Mom said. "I'm sure he's a nice man and he means well, but you've gotten so intense, Hana. It scares me."

"What did he say?"

"Well, of course he denied—I mean, I didn't accuse him of anything exactly, but—Hana! Oh, honey, I didn't mean to embarrass you. I'm sorry. I just wanted to make sure—"

"I wish I was dead," Hana cried. "Now I can't even say good-bye to him."

Mom brought her hands up to her cheeks dramatically. "What's happened to you? It's not like you to be this emotional, Hana. You've turned into a teenager overnight and you're only twelve."

"What've birth dates got to do with it, Mom? People grow up when they have to," Hana said coldly.

"Hana!" Mom rebuked her. "Since when do you talk to me that way?"

"What way? I just made a true statement." She went to her bedroom, shut the door behind her, and lay down. Everything had become a horrible mess. The most wonderful experience of her life had been turned into slime by her family. They were awful, every one of them, even Mom.

Mom sent Eric in to tell her they were leaving to go to a movie, but Hana refused to go, even though it was a comedy she had wanted to see. Before, they would have made her go, but tonight Mom wasn't pressuring her. Even Elena didn't come into the bedroom to goad her. Alan was building something in the basement, whistling as he worked, and behaving as if staying home were his own idea instead of the result of his being grounded. Dad was still off fishing. So only Eric and Elena went to the movie with Mom.

Hana got a pad and a pen. She was going to write a letter to David to apologize for the embarrassment her mother must have caused him and to beg him not to let it get in the way of his decision. Not all parents were as ridiculous as hers. He could be a teacher and handle kids if he just pretended to be meaner and didn't let them get away with anything. She started giving examples.

Last spring he'd let Mike sit next to his girlfriend and hold her hand because they'd finished their work early. But then everyone else in class started watching what Mike and his girlfriend were doing instead of paying attention to their own work. Another time, Mr. Crane had laughed when Vinnie got down on his hands and knees and clowned around begging for forgiveness because he'd lost his homework assignment. And he never realized the noise level was going up until it was way too high to bring back down. By the time Hana had finished three pages, she reread what she'd written and was struck by how negative her letter sounded. He'd never go back to teaching after reading it. She ripped the letter up.

"Dear Mr. Crane," she began again. "I'm sorry about my mother's misunderstanding. She misunderstands everything, so don't feel you're the only one. I know you're a grown man and I'm a kid, and you've been kind to me just because you're a kind person. The way I feel, though—" No, she wouldn't write that she loved him. What could she say? "I'm just glad to have spent some time with you this week. It meant a lot to me, because I think you're a very deep and beautiful person."

She was on the fourth attempt at a letter when she gave up. She would have to go and say good-bye to him in person. Alan would tell on her, though, if he noticed she was gone. The thing to do was wait until the family was asleep and then sneak out of the house and knock on David's door. At night? No, she'd better wait until morning. But if she waited till then, someone in the family would be up and she'd never get out without their knowing. Yes, she would, if she could will herself to wake up early enough. Five o'clock maybe, before even Alan got up to run.

Very well, then, she would wake up before dawn. Once she made up her mind to do something, she always did it.

Chapter 9

It was one of those evenings when the family couldn't seem to go to bed. The moviegoers returned by nine-thirty—Hana could hear them in the kitchen foraging for snacks. And then Alan's voice. Still pretending he was home by choice, he suggested with a show of great enthusiasm that they play poker. Mom sounded sympathetic when she said that would be fun and why didn't they all play. Of course, Mom would be sympathetic, Hana thought. Mom knew how hard it was for her most restless child to be grounded. But a poker night could last for hours! In dismay, Hana got up and went to the kitchen to see what was happening.

Dad had come back fishless and grouchy, but he liked poker. He sat himself down at the kitchen table with a deck of cards and a grunt of satisfaction. Elena and Eric migrated to the table the minute Dad began shuffling.

"Come on, baby, I'll stake you," Mom said when she spotted Hana in the doorway. The family habit was to play for pennies, and it was possible to lose a dollar or more in an evening.

"I have my own money, but I don't feel like playing," Hana said.

"She's mad at us," Elena said.

"What for?" Dad asked.

"Because Mom interfered with her love life," Elena said.

"I'm reading," Hana said. In despair she returned to her bedroom to reimmerse herself in her book. She had finished the last thirty pages and could still hear the family out there in the kitchen bantering with one another. Sometimes they'd stay up past midnight playing poker. Hana hoped tonight wasn't going to be one of those times.

She was of two minds about poker. On the one hand, she'd always liked that the family had this game they could enjoy together, and she'd learned to play when she was seven. On the other hand, she'd never been good at gambling. No matter how often her father instructed her about the odds of turning up a particular card, she would bet too much on the hope of filling an inside straight, and she could never make herself throw in her cards early on a losing hand. She hoped for the unlikely and felt personally defeated when it didn't happen. Poker was painful for her. So was waiting for her family to go to bed tonight.

Laughter came from the kitchen. It was past eleven. If the cottage wasn't so small that there was no way to sneak out of it without being seen, she could go speak to David now. Of course, he might be in bed asleep. She didn't know if he was a night person or a day person. There was so much she didn't know about him, so much she'd like to ask if she had the time. Well, she didn't, but she had to see him again before he left the Cape, if only to release him from the curse her mother had put on him.

Imagine him sitting alone and thinking that he came out wrong even with a student like her, whom he'd thought he could count on! That would surely convince him that he was a failure as a teacher. And if his career decision resulted from the misunderstandings of her overprotective family, the blame would be hers. She, Hana, would have caused him to give up teaching.

Oh, David, she whispered into the dark. Being too young to do as she wanted was an affliction, a crippling disease. It would be so simple to go to him and straighten things out. But her parents didn't want her to see him anymore. And she could barely move a muscle without their permission.

If she were old enough—eighteen maybe—she could go off to college and there he'd be. He would have become a college professor. He wouldn't have aged, and he'd never have married, and when she introduced herself to him, he'd remember who she was. His face would light up as he said her name, "Hana!"

She'd just smile.

He'd say, "I've thought of you often and wondered about you. I see you've grown up beautiful." And his gaze would be melting with admiration.

She would take his writing course and they would meet at a coffee shop to discuss what she had written. It would be something deep that would impress him, like about how strong the bond could be between people who put nature and books ahead of any other interests.

"I never felt as close to any member of my family as I did to you," she would tell him.

"If only you hadn't been so young, I might have let myself fall in love with you," David would say.

"I'm not so young anymore," she would tell him.

And would he lean toward her and kiss her then? *Ummm*, Hana thought and closed her eyes to dream about the touch of his lips. She was smiling as she fell asleep.

───────

She woke up at dawn when the world outside belonged to a choir of birds. Inside, the cottage was so still she had a hard time believing it held five other people. Elena made a silent hillock under her comforter in the bed beside Hana's. Then bedsprings creaked as someone turned over and someone male spoke in his sleep.

Hana tiptoed to the bathroom, carrying her thongs and shorts and T-shirt to put on there. She studied her tanned oval face in its frame of straight brown hair and thought again that if her eyes were larger or her lips fuller or her cheekbones higher, she might be pretty. But she was ordinary looking. Nothing special outside or in. It was no wonder her family had no respect for her.

She brushed her teeth and ran a comb through her hair. Ever so carefully, she let herself out the front door, holding the screen door until it shut softly behind her. Finally she was free to walk down the road to David's apartment.

A tinge of pink showed over the cove where the

sun was rising above the bluffs. The sky was pale and vast; the water in the cove was silvered over and the air was dewy. She felt a buzz of hope. Perhaps he wasn't totally disgusted with her. Perhaps he would forgive her.

She climbed the wooden stairs to his room off the deck over the garage, feeling more anxious with every step. What if he were still sleeping? Of course he would be. Who was up this early but the birds and one early-morning dog walker? She was crazy. David would think she was, anyway.

The curtain had been left open and so had the sliding glass door, to allow air through the screen. She could see him sprawled on the single bed across from the door, asleep with the sheet wound round his slim body. She teetered on the top step, afraid to advance and unwilling to retreat. Better wait for him to wake up, but suppose he slept late? Her mother would send out a posse to lynch David Crane if she found her daughter here. No matter that he was totally innocent and Hana had come of her own accord. They'd never believe that because she was a *child*.

A note, then. She should have written that note. She considered returning to the cottage and starting all over again to explain everything to him on paper. No doubt the family would sleep late after staying up past midnight. Dad would get up by seven, though. He always did. And what if she didn't get the note done in time and was trapped in the cottage?

Get up, she willed silently. Get up now, David.

Miraculously, as if he'd been summoned, he yawned and rolled to a sitting position. He rubbed his eyes and stood up. He was wearing boxer shorts. She turned her head the other way so that she wouldn't seem to be spying on him.

"Hana!" he said, sliding the door all the way open. "What are you doing here?"

"I came to apologize. And to say good-bye." He had a sheet wrapped around him like a toga. Yes, he looked like a noble Roman.

"And I bet your family doesn't know where you are," he said. The idea seemed to scare him because he frowned at her.

"It's all right. They're sleeping in this morning."

"But Hana, your mother is already"—he hesitated, searching for a word—"uncomfortable with us spending time alone together. I think you had better get home."

"Just let me tell you—please."

"Tell me what?"

"That you shouldn't let my stupid family mess up your life. I mean, if you want to try teaching again, you should, because you aren't going to get into trouble just for being nice to a kid—not with anybody but my stupid parents."

"Hey," he said. "Don't be down on them. They're just trying to protect you. I mean, for all they know, I could be—what they suspect. After all, it's unusual for a guy my age to enjoy the company of a girl your age. It's—but you were so good to talk to, and I felt you understood."

"I do understand. And I think you're wonderful. I think you can do any job in the world you want to."

He laughed. "Think I could be a wrestler, hmm?" He flexed his muscleless arms. "Or a mathematician? I'm terrible at math, which is something you don't know about me. I'm not much of an athlete either, actually."

"But you could be any of those things you talked about wanting to do."

A cardinal landed on the porch railing and they both turned to admire its scarlet accent against the dove gray of morning. When the bird flew off, he said, "You're sweet, Hana, and I appreciate that you're concerned about me. But don't worry. I'll be fine. What's really important is for you to realize that you're lucky to have a such a solid family."

"You wouldn't think you were so lucky if you were me."

"Listen, nobody thinks their parents understand them at your age. I sure didn't."

"I'm just the afterthought in my family."

"I doubt that, Hana," he said. "They love you. I mean, if you were my sister, I'd love you. You're just mad at them because they read our relationship wrong. That's all."

She bit her lip. "I could have died when I heard my mother actually came here to yell at you. I'm so sorry, Mr. Crane."

"Yeah, well, she shook me up a little, but she didn't yell. And I think I convinced her that we're just friends. Of course—" He waggled his eyebrows up and down in a comic attempt to show nervousness. "We'd have a hard time reconvincing her if she found you hanging out with me at dawn."

"I'm leaving. I'll just tell them I went for a walk."

"No, don't lie. Tell them you came to say good-bye."

"I did. I did want to say good-bye." Tears began dripping down her cheeks. She swiped at them hastily.

"Listen, Hana," he said tenderly. "It was great being with you this week. You made me feel a whole lot better about myself. You're a very special person. Remember that, okay?"

"Thanks," she croaked and turned to go.

He stood watching as if he were concerned about her.

At the bottom of the stairs she realized she didn't know whether he was going to return to teaching or not. She wiped her tears with the back of her hand and called up to him. "Mr. Crane?"

He leaned over the stair railing so that all she could see was his head and his bare arms. "Yeah?"

"Are you going back to teaching?"

"I don't think so." He held up his hand as if he were taking an oath. "Not because of your mother. Really, Hana. I just think maybe I have to do some growing up myself before I try teaching again."

She nodded. "Well, good luck."

"Good luck to you," he said. "And Hana?"

"Yes?"

"I'd adopt you as my little sister any day."

It wasn't what she wanted to hear, but she thanked him politely and left. She cried so hard walking back to the cottage that she could barely see the road.

They were all still asleep. She curled up on the couch and leaked hot tears onto Grandma's fat chintz cushions. It was over. The most wonderful experience of her life was over, and her family hadn't understood one bit of it.

Worse yet, Mr. Crane hadn't understood, either.

She was sure it was because she didn't match inside and out. Inside she was grown up, but outside she looked like a child. That had to be why he didn't see that the last thing she wanted to be was his sister.

Chapter 10

"What's the matter with you, Hana?" Mom asked. She and Hana were the only ones at the breakfast table.

"Nothing." Hana stopped toying with her cereal and gripped the spoon as if it would give her strength.

"You've been crying, haven't you?"

"Yes."

"What about?"

"I went to say good-bye to Mr. Crane this morning."

"Hana! Why did you do that?"

"Because I didn't want him not to be a teacher because of us."

"Oh, honey. I told you I didn't accuse him of anything. I really didn't. All I said was that I thought you were too young to be spending so much time with him."

"And that's not accusing him of anything?"

"Hana—"

"You were wrong, Mom. You shouldn't have barged in. Even if I do love him, he only likes me back. And he made me feel good, which is something nobody in this family does."

She left the cereal half eaten and escaped to her room then, despite Mom's pleading cry of "Haaana!"

Elena was still asleep, cocooned in her quilt with her feet sticking out from the bottom and her hair spilling over the top. Hana returned her own body to the hollow center of her unmade bed. She pulled the pillow over her head for privacy and only peeked out from under it a long time later when someone touched her shoulder.

"I just wanted to say I'm sorry," Eric said. He perched on the edge of her bed as if he were unsure of his welcome and ready to make a quick getaway.

"What for?"

"Well," he exhaled lengthily, "I think you do get the short end of the stick from us a lot of times. And you are a pretty good kid. Anyway, I'm planning on treating you as if you might be human from now on."

"You are? Thanks, Eric."

He nodded, his solemn face satisfied with their exchange. "So if you want me to drive you to the library or something, just let me know, okay?"

"Okay," she said, and dove back under her pillow.

Next came an arm slung across her body. Hana rolled over and bopped Elena with the pillow. "What do you want?"

"I want you to like me again," Elena said.

Hana pulled the pillow away to see if Elena was mocking her. She didn't look as if she were mocking. In fact, her eyes were brimming with real tears.

"I've been thinking, and I guess you've got a point," Elena said. "I do sort of bully you sometimes. And I don't talk to you the way I talk to my friends, I mean about my personal life."

"No, you don't."

"Well, so, you want to start?"

"Being friends?"

"Yeah, in a way," Elena said. "I mean, you're getting old enough to be more than a pest, and I guess if your teacher can talk to you, I can. After all, I'm your sister."

"You are. So talk." Hana sat up, with her legs crossed under her, and leaned her chin on her fist to listen.

"All right." Elena looked uncomfortable, but she plunged in. "So you know how I told Mom and Dad

I hated coming to Grandma's place and next summer I was going to get a job and stay in town?"

"Yeah."

"Well, that was because Rob said he wanted to stop going steady with me while I was gone so he could be free to see other girls."

"I know."

"What do you mean, you know?"

"Your friend Dee told me."

"Oh. So you understand why I haven't been too happy?"

"But you didn't have to take it out on me."

"No. But if I'm mean to Alan, he's meaner back. And Eric just ignores me. And Mom always makes me feel bad when I'm mean to her. You know how she does it."

Hana nodded.

"And you can't be mean to Dad or he'll ground you," Elena concluded.

"Why do you have to be mean at all?"

"Being unhappy makes me mean."

"Well, being the youngest is the pits," Hana said with passion.

Elena considered. "Mmm. You know, I used to think you got off easy as the baby, but I guess you do have problems. . . . So tell me about Mr. Crane."

"He's nice, and he made me feel like a person, but we were just friends."

"Uh huh. But you do love him, don't you?"

Hana burst into tears. Elena took her into her arms and rubbed her back comfortingly, the way Mom used to when Hana was sick. It felt good. Then Elena kissed her and said, "I'm going to the beach. Want to come with me?"

"No, thanks. Not yet," Hana said.

"Okay, I'll see you later then." Elena waved and wafted out of the room as if she'd rid herself of a heavy load.

Mom was the next visitor. She plunked down heavily on the bed next to Hana, making it sag so that Hana slid against her mother's warm body.

"Hana, I'm sorry. I suppose I did overreact about Mr. Crane. You read so much in the papers. I'm sorry if I upset you. But I'm sure that young man isn't going to base his life decisions on anything I said. So you don't need to worry about that. . . . Do you forgive me?"

Hana couldn't remember her mother ever seriously asking for her forgiveness before. She sat up straight and stared at Mom.

"Believe me, when you have children of your own, you'll understand," Mom went on. "It's so hard to keep your kids safe, especially when they grow up. And you're growing up a lot faster than I expected."

Mom bit her lip and looked so miserable Hana couldn't stand it. She patted her mother's hands. "Okay," she said. "Don't worry. Actually, even if you did convince him not to be a teacher, it might be better. Because I don't think he's ready to be a good one yet."

Mom brushed Hana's hair back from her face and held her chin. "You're getting to be such a pretty girl. I hope you have more sense about boys than Elena does."

"I'm pretty sensible," Hana said.

Mom smiled. "I used to think so. I need one daughter I can rely on not to do anything foolish behind my back."

Hana wasn't so sure she wouldn't do anything foolish, but she promised she wouldn't, and Mom seemed relieved. "Are you and Mr. Crane going to keep in touch?" Mom asked before she left the room.

"I don't think so," Hana said. After all, he wasn't likely to write to her, and she didn't know where he'd be so she couldn't write to him. Probably he didn't know where he'd be, either.

"Too bad," Mom said as if she didn't really mean it. "Well, come and eat something. You'll feel better with some food in you."

Hana wondered if Alan and her father would come to her bedroom, too, if she waited long enough. Since that was extremely unlikely, and she was hungry, she got up and went to the kitchen. Alan was baking another cake. Dad was just turning off the TV news in the living room.

"You know, Dad," Alan said. "I've been thinking. Is it just because Hana's the youngest and a girl that she gets away with murder?"

"What?" Dad barked.

"I got grounded for not being where I was supposed to be. Mom said Hana ran off to meet the guy she was told not to see, and *nothing* happens to her. How come?"

Hana couldn't believe the way Alan was trying to use her. But on second thought, she could. "Alan, you're a rat," she said.

"That's all right, Hana," her father said. "Your brother's not going to get you in trouble."

"Because she's just a little kid, right?" Alan finished for Dad. "But she's not a little kid if she's old enough to get hung up on an older guy."

"She's not hung up on any older guy except me," Dad roared as if yelling it loud enough could make it true.

"Hana, do you love your teacher?" Alan asked.

"Yes," she said defiantly.

"See, Dad?"

"Fine," Dad said. "Then she's grounded, too. Does that make you happy, Alan?"

"In a democratic country, the length of a prison sentence is supposed to match the crime. Can you at least tell me how long I'm grounded for?" Alan asked.

"For the rest of your life," Dad snapped. "And I don't want to hear another word out of you this morning."

"I think," Mom said, "that we should all go to the beach today."

"Even the grounded family members?" Alan asked.

"Alan!" Dad thundered.

"It will do us all good," Mom said. "I'll pack a picnic lunch . . . and how about we go out to Great Island? The fishing's good there, isn't it, Vergil?"

Dad scrunched up his jowly face and nodded. "Yah, okay," he said, and he went to get his fishing tackle ready.

"Wow!" Alan said. "I didn't know you had that much power, Mom."

"There's a lot you don't know about your own family," Mom said.

Alan smiled. "Good timing. This cake's just about baked. I can frost it tonight when it's cooled. What do you say, Hana, lemon or cocoa?"

"Lemon," she said. It was her favorite and he never made it because he was a chocolate freak.

"Done," he said.

That was almost as good as if he'd come to her room; at least it was the best she was likely to get from Alan.

———

It was low tide at Great Island that morning. The family walked in a clump like an amoeba stretching out in one direction and another, forming pairs and threesomes and breaking apart again along the uninhabited miles of empty beach. They searched for shells and rocks and occasionally swam out into the bay between sand bars to cool off.

Hana collected a plastic bag full of orange and black and brown and white scallop shells, each one slightly different in color and pattern from the next. Elena found white stones that were either perfectly round or egg-like, or sculptured by the waves into the shape of a seal or a sleeping bird or a whale. Alan skipped stones and yelled with pleasure when he beat his best past performance with one that touched the water fourteen times before it sank.

Eric's foot got sliced by a razor clam shell he stepped on accidentally. He hobbled along comically fast on the heel of his right foot, trying to keep up with the rest of the family. Mom's nose turned bright red from the sun. Dad told them a story about their grandfather, who had been bitten by a shark as a young man and never went swimming again the rest of his long life.

"Shark attacks are rarer than airplane accidents. He shouldn't have given up swimming," Alan said.

"Just couldn't make himself relax in the water after that. Not even in a pool," Dad said. "It's all in your head. Everything's in your head."

On the way home, Dad was walking just in front of Eric, who was limping along, and behind Alan and Elena, who were insulting each other in amiable competition. Hana dropped back from Mom so that Dad could catch up with her if he felt like being with his wife, but he slowed his steps and walked alongside Hana.

"When you were a little tyke," he said, "you used to come fishing with me, and you'd sit there for hours keeping me company. I liked that."

"You did?" she said. "I never thought you noticed I was there."

"I noticed," he said. "You're easy to be around, Hana, not a pest like Alan and Elena, or a sad sack like your brother Eric."

"Thank you, Daddy."

"You know," he said, "when we had you, your mother and I weren't too thrilled because we thought we'd finished having kids. They take a lot out of you, let me tell you." He grunted and nodded to himself. Then he added, "But you turned out to be just the little girl we'd always wanted."

"I did?"

"Still are," he said, and he gave her an awkward hug that nearly knocked her over.

It took Hana a minute to recover from her amazement. By then Dad had caught up with Mom and was walking beside her. Alone for the first time that morning, Hana smiled to herself. Mr. Crane had been right when he said she was lucky to have such a solid family. He had seen what she'd been blind to. She might not be ready for a grown-up love relationship yet, but she certainly had potential as a sister and as a daughter.

She smiled again, thinking of how disappointed she'd felt when Mr. Crane had said he wished she could be his sister. What an awful mess it would have been if he'd wanted something different from her. So he'd handled that situation well. Chalk up one for Mr. Crane. Fervently she hoped he would find a job he was good at. She only wished he hadn't gone before she realized how much she had to thank him for. Because as things turned out, he had done as much for her, or more, than she had done for him.

"Wait for me," she yelled now to her family. "Wait for meee!" And she ran as hard as she could to catch up with them.